The Leopard in the Golden Cage

Julia Edwards was born in 1977. She lives in Salisbury with her husband and three sons, and sometimes feels outnumbered.

The Leopard in the Golden Cage is the first book in *The Scar Gatherer* series, a sequence of seven adventure novels about time-travel.

To find out more, please visit: *www.scargatherer.co.uk*.

Also by Julia Edwards

Other titles in The Scar Gatherer series

Saving the Unicorn's Horn

The Falconer's Quarry

The Demon in the Embers

Slaves for the Isabella

The Shimmer on the Glass

The Ring from the Ruins

For adults

Time was Away

THE FIRST BOOK IN The Scar Gatherer SERIES

The Leopard
in the
Golden Cage

Julia Edwards

Published in the United Kingdom by:

Laverstock Publishing
129 Church Road, Laverstock, Salisbury,
Wiltshire, SP1 1RB, UK

First printed March 2014
Revised edition printed October 2019

Cover design by Peter O'Connor
www.bespokebookcovers.com

ISBN: 978-0-9928443-0-1

For more information about the series, please visit
www.scargatherer.co.uk

For the children who read
the very first Leopard and told me
what they thought of it!

ACKNOWLEDGEMENTS

First and foremost, I would like to thank my husband for making it possible for me to pursue my literary ambitions. Thanks also to my parents for investing their faith and money in my venture! I am also grateful to them and to the friends and many children who read earlier versions of the book and helped me to improve on it. The guide at Fishbourne Roman Palace one quiet January day was both informative and patient in answering my many questions; and his colleague, Katrina Burton kindly checked my facts and corrected my errors. Any errors that remain are my own.

1

Joe sat at the kitchen table and stared out of the window, his chin on his hand.

"Hurry up," said his mum. "The others will be here soon. We need to get ready to go."

"It's not fair," Joe grumbled. "How come Sam gets to take a friend and I don't?"

"We can't fit anyone else in the car. You can take someone next time we go out for the day."

Joe went back to eating his cornflakes. Ben was Sam's best friend, and his mum, Kate, was Mum's best friend. So both Sam and Mum would be taking their friends. It was just Joe who would be on his own.

He went upstairs to brush his teeth, wishing that Dad was coming with them. Today was the first day of the summer holidays. In nineteen days, Joe and Sam were going to stay with Dad for a week. Joe knew it wasn't fair on Mum to be looking forward to it so much, but he couldn't help it. As for the other five weeks, the thought of them filled him with misery.

He rinsed his hands under the tap and ran them through his hair. It was blond and a little bit wavy, and it stuck up with the water. He flattened it down and peered at himself in the mirror. There was nothing special about him that would ever make him stand out - hazel eyes, average height, neither skinny nor fat. He would be eleven in September. Sam, who was thirteen, was loads taller. Joe sighed. One day, he would catch up with his brother.

The doorbell rang.

"Hurry up, please, Joe!" his mum called from the foot of the stairs.

It was crowded on the back seat of the car, with Sam, Ben and Joe all squeezed in together. They drove for what seemed like a long time.

"How much further?" Joe asked eventually.

"Not long now."

"Where are we going, again?"

"It's called Fishbourne Roman Palace," said Kate. "There was once a huge villa there. We're going to look at the ruins, and the museum."

"Sounds a bit boring," said Ben.

"It won't be," Kate said. "They've got some amazing mosaics - you know, those floors made of thousands of tiny tiles. They're really, really old. There's one that's quite famous, a boy riding a dolphin."

Joe looked out of the window at the passing trees and houses. Normally, he liked ruined castles and that kind of thing. But normally, they went with Dad who told such incredibly vivid stories about places that you felt like you'd actually been there.

They drove through a housing estate and came to a barrier on a road.

"Here we are, then! The gateway to the palace!" Joe's mum said, in that falsely bright voice she used so often at the moment.

They paid for their tickets at the entrance. "There's a film about the palace," said the lady at the ticket desk. "I suggest you start by watching that. It'll give you an idea of what you're looking at."

Joe followed his mum and Kate into the auditorium. It was very dark. He sat down at the end of the row and hunched his shoulders. Sam and Ben whispered and sniggered together.

The film was sort of interesting, Joe thought, with its computer graphics showing what the palace might have looked like. But when they stepped out into the daylight again, he was disappointed to see that half of it was now underneath the backs of houses all around. In fact, there was only half of the garden and the floor of one section of the palace left. He wished he could wave a magic wand and make it all reappear.

"Let's go and have a look at the mosaics," Mum said.

Joe trailed after her. Sam and Ben larked around, their feet booming on the wooden walkways.

"Here it is!" called Sam. "Here's the famous

one!" His voice echoed beneath the high ceiling of the museum building.

"Look at that!" Kate leaned on the rail. "Isn't it beautiful?"

Joe went along the walkway on the other side from them. If Dad had been here, he would have been describing the man laying the mosaic, crawling around with his trays of tile fragments and his plan, grumbling about his stiff back or his sore knees, or his apprentice making the mortar too sloppy so that the tiles slipped.

Joe reached inside the neck of his T-shirt to touch the St. Christopher Dad had given him just before he moved out. He held it between his finger and thumb, pressing it hard, as though he could conjure Dad out of thin air. Nothing happened, of course. He looked down at it. But the chain it was on was too short for him to really see it. Without thinking, he gave it a tug. There was a snapping sound. The chain slithered down around his neck. He fumbled to catch it, but as he did so, the St. Christopher slipped from his fingers. There was a tinkling sound as it bounced on the mosaic floor. Then it rolled away beneath the walkway.

"Oh, no!" he cried out.

"What's the matter?" His mum turned back towards him from the next mosaic.

"I've dropped my St. Christopher!"

"Silly boy!" Joe could tell that Mum was annoyed, even though she was pretending not to be.

"We'll have to ask if someone can get it for you."

For the next five minutes, there was a lot of fuss while Joe's mum asked at the ticket desk, and the ticket desk sent someone off to find someone else. Joe leaned out over the rail as far as he could, trying desperately to see the St. Christopher, embarrassed at the trouble he'd caused.

The guide came along and climbed down from the walkway, tiptoeing around the edge of the mosaic. "I can't see anything." He got down on his hands and knees. "You do mean a little silver disk, a bit smaller than a ten-pence piece?"

Joe nodded.

The guide crawled around the edge of the floor. "It doesn't seem to be on the mosaic, but I can't see it under the walkway either."

After another minute, he stood up. "I'm really sorry, young man, but I'm afraid it's well and truly disappeared. No sign of the chain either. Maybe they've got caught in your clothes."

Joe swallowed. He knew they hadn't.

"Never mind, darling." His mum put her arm around him. "We'll have to get you another one."

He hung his head. Another one wouldn't be the same. And what was he going to tell Dad?

"Let's go and have something to eat."

But Joe was dejected as he ate his packed lunch. "I need to go to the loo," he said, after a few minutes.

"Well, you know where we are," Mum said. "We

won't go anywhere without you."

Back inside the museum, Joe went straight to where he had dropped the St. Christopher. It simply had to be there somewhere. It wasn't possible that it had disappeared!

He looked all around. There were a couple of families down at the far end of the building, but most people had gone off for lunch. If he was really quick, he might get away with having a look for himself.

After glancing around one more time, he slipped through the rails and dropped down on to the mosaic.

There was a hissing sound, like air escaping from a punctured tyre. It was probably some kind of air-conditioning, he thought. He crawled forward on his hands and knees beneath the walkway. He'd had the impression before that there were lights underneath, shining across the mosaic, but now that he was down here, it seemed quite dark. There was a big piece of furniture under here too, a heavy wooden sideboard of some kind.

The edges of the tiles were slightly rough against his palm. The design on this side of the picture looked different close up to how it had looked from above. He frowned. He was sure there had been swirling circles before. But beneath his hands was a square zigzag design, like the battlements of a castle. In the dim light, it looked black and white rather than coloured. He swept his hand along underneath the sideboard. There was a lot of dust, but he couldn't feel his St. Christopher.

"What are you doing?"

Joe jumped guiltily to his feet. The room seemed to rush in on him. He swayed and blinked. The museum had vanished. The dolphin mosaic had vanished too. He stood on a black and white floor in a much smaller room.

"Don't worry! I won't bite." A girl with dark hair stood in the doorway. She was wearing a long, pale dress and sandals. Joe stared. A few moments before, there had been no doorway. There had been no walls in which to have a doorway. Now there were walls and a ceiling, a couch, a low table, and on one side, a small kind of wood-burner. The room was dim. Apart from the doorway, the only light came from windows with greenish-blue glass at the top of the walls.

"Who are you?" he asked.

"I should be asking you that! I live here. You don't."

"Really? You live here? In a museum?"

The girl laughed. "It's not a museum! It's a palace. And I am Sallustia Lucilia, second daughter of Gaius Sallustius Lucullus."

"Who's he when he's at home?" Joe asked.

She looked shocked. "He is the owner of this palace and the Propraetorian Imperial Legate to the Emperor Domitian himself." She drew herself up tall.

"What's a property-imperial-whatever-it-was?"

Joe frowned.

The girl stuck her nose in the air. "He's the governor of Britannia, the most important man in the land. And I am his daughter."

Joe shook his head. "You can't be. Are you here for some kind of fancy dress day?"

"What's fancy dress?" She dropped her haughty manner.

Joe pointed at her costume. "Those clothes. You look like you're dressed up."

She smoothed her skirt with her hands. "This is my best dress, actually. We've got visitors coming, so my mother wanted us all to look nice."

"Oh. Right." Joe could hear that he sounded unfriendly, but it irritated him that she was pretending not to understand him. "What I mean is, nobody wears that kind of thing normally. Most people wear this kind of -" He glanced down at himself to indicate his shorts and T-shirt. But the clothes he'd put on this morning had completely changed. He was wearing a loose tunic with a belt around the middle, and leather sandals similar to the girl's ones. He touched the fabric of the tunic. It felt real enough, smooth rather than scratchy, like a kind of heavy cotton. He gaped at it. "What's going on?"

"Nothing's going on!" she said. "Are you one of my cousins? We're expecting a lot of people, but I didn't think any of them had arrived."

"No. I'm Joe." He hesitated, then said, "Well, in

fact I'm Joseph Edward Hopkins."

"That's a funny name."

"No it's not!" Joe was indignant. "It's your name that's strange! What did you say it was?"

"Sallustia Lucilia," she repeated, primly.

"Sallustia?" He wrinkled his nose. "I've never heard that before. Don't people call you Sally for short?"

She gave him a look, as though he had asked a stupid question. "Nobody calls me either Sallustia or Sally, but there's nothing strange about the name. Both of my sisters are called Sallustia as well. My older sister is Sallustia Domitia. She's nearly fourteen. And my younger sister is Sallustia Antonia. She's eight. I'm ten."

"Me too," said Joe. "Though I'll be eleven soon," he added hastily. "Isn't it a bit confusing if you all have the same name?"

"Of course not!" the girl said. "Only my older sister is actually called Sallustia. My little sister is Antonia and I'm Lucilia."

"Lucilia," Joe repeated. "That's still a bit of a frilly name. Can I call you Lucy?"

The girl looked doubtful. "If you must," she said, pursing her lips. "Anyway, you still haven't answered my first question. What were you doing when I came in?"

"I was looking for something I dropped earlier, my St. Christopher."

"What's that?"

"It's like a medallion. You wear it round your neck. St. Christopher is the patron saint of travellers so it's supposed to keep you safe if you're travelling."

"A bit like this?" Her hand went to her throat. On a leather thong around her neck hung a circular gold pendant. It had curved surfaces that reminded Joe of a sherbet flying saucer.

"This bulla belonged to my brother," she said. "When he died, they were going to bury it with him. But they decided to give it to me instead."

Joe's mouth fell open. If Sam died, he couldn't imagine talking about it in such a matter of fact way.

"They're to ward off evil spirits," she went on.

"You don't believe in that kind of thing, do you?" Joe said.

Her eyes widened. "Of course! In fact, now I think about it, you could be an evil spirit. You're obviously not my cousin, and how else have you appeared here out of the blue?"

"I didn't appear out of the blue," he said crossly. "I came with my mum and my brother and their friends..." He stopped. He'd come to the museum with them, but this wasn't a museum any more. His mind struggled to get a grip on what was happening to him. It was impossible! More than that, it was completely unbelievable! But there was no other way to explain it. He seemed to have slipped through time.

"Well, never mind," Lucy said. "If you're a

spirit, perhaps you're a good one. But even so, you shouldn't be in here. I shouldn't be in here either. These rooms are for guests. We live over on the other side. Shall I show you?"

She put her head out into the corridor and looked both ways, then drew herself up sharply against the wall. "There's someone coming," she whispered. "We'll have to hide." She looked around in a panic. "I'll be in such trouble if I get caught!" She darted round behind the couch. "You, too!" she hissed.

Joe could hear the footsteps outside now. Despite Lucy's obvious anxiety, he found it hard to be worried. It was all so unreal.

"Get down!" Lucy grabbed the hem of his tunic and pulled him down behind the couch next to her.

The doorway darkened as someone walked into the room. Joe wanted to peep out and see who it was. Lucy shook her head silently. The footsteps retreated.

Joe stood up. There was now a huge bowl of fruit on the table. He went over and picked up a peach. It was soft and downy, just like at home, but it smelled like the ripest, sweetest peach he had ever eaten. He was about to bite into it when Lucy caught hold of his arm.

"What are you doing? Put it back! We need to get out of here!" Her face was pale. "Come on, before anyone else comes! That was only a slave. Next time, it'll be my mother, coming to see if everything's ready for the guests."

Reluctantly, Joe put the peach back in the bowl and followed her out across the corridor, through a courtyard, and into a kind of cloister with pillars and a roof.

"Right." Lucy's colour had come back into her cheeks. "We need to decide what on earth to do with you."

2

They walked quickly along the cloister in front of the north wing of the palace, and then down the eastern cloister.

"Why can't we just go straight across the garden?" Joe asked. "That would be much quicker."

"We can't walk there!" Lucy said, scandalised. "We'd be noticed. Only my parents walk there, and then only when they have important visitors."

"You're not allowed to play in the garden?"

"Of course we are. Just not this one. This is the formal garden. There would be no point going into it, even if we were allowed to. You can see there's nowhere to hide, and the cypress trees wouldn't be much fun to climb. These espaliers wouldn't be any good either, and the gardeners would be furious. We have other gardens on the side where we live. We can do what we like there."

Joe looked around as he followed her. It was so hard to take in. He felt like his brain was still shouting at him all the time, that this couldn't be real, there must be some kind of trick or optical illusion or something like that. Perhaps he was in a film set. But that didn't explain the way this other world had sprung up around him, in a fraction of a second. And it didn't explain the fact that the modern houses he'd wanted to magic away earlier had genuinely disappeared.

Time travel didn't happen, not in real life, he told himself. But the alcoves in the hedges now had statues and fountains in them, just like they'd said in the information film. And around the sections of hedged lawn was a whole palace just like the computer simulation he'd seen earlier.

It was a series of big low buildings like four sides of a square, with roofs made with large red tiles, like something out of Italy. Along each side of the square there was a covered cloister - colonnades, he remembered they were called - and they were all the same, except for the one on the west side which was grander. He wished he'd paid more attention to the model in the museum earlier on. Then he would have known what the different parts of the palace were supposed to be for, assuming the archaeologists had got it right.

Of course, he could always ask Lucy. But at the moment, he felt he would rather not ask her more than he had to. In any case, he thought, the archaeologists seemed to have done pretty well with their reconstruction. They'd be pleased if they knew.

Suddenly, he wondered whether one of them had been here and had a look, like he was doing now. That would explain how they'd managed to get so much of it right. After all, if he really had slipped through time by mistake himself, why shouldn't someone else have done the same? Maybe there was some kind of hole in the air, like an invisible doorway.

But he hadn't noticed anything when he climbed through the rail to look for his St. Christopher. He was just in the present one moment, and here - wherever here was - the next. It was completely baffling. This other world felt just as real as his own. But everything looked different.

As they stepped out of the shade of the colonnade at the end of the east wing, he realised that there was something else that was different too. Back at home, it had been cloudy and cool. Here, it was really hot, in a way it never was at home, more like it had been when they went on holiday to Italy last summer.

"What's in there?" he asked, pointing to a building with curved roofs on the end of the east wing.

"That's the bath house," Lucy said. "We go there once a week."

Joe remembered the pictures of Roman baths he'd seen in books at school. They looked like swimming pools. "Can we go there?"

Lucy was shocked. "Not together! It's men and boys in the afternoon. I go in the mornings with the women."

"That's a pity. It would be nice to cool off."

She looked surprised. "It's warm today, I suppose, but it gets quite a bit hotter than this. Where *do* you come from?"

Joe didn't answer. He didn't know what to say.

Beyond the bath house was another garden. This was quite different from the formal garden in the centre of the palace. Here, there were bushes and trees, many of them of kinds that he didn't recognise, dotted around an enormous lawn. The lawn itself ran the full length of the south wing and further, sloping down towards the sea. There were flowers too, in huge flowerbeds like in a park back at home.

"Is all this yours?" He gazed around. "You could get lost here!"

Lucy beamed. "It's wonderful, isn't it? We only moved here last year. It took quite a while before the palace was ready for us, but it was worth the wait. It's much nicer than where we lived before."

"Where was that?"

She frowned vaguely. "I'm not sure. Somewhere near Verulamium I think."

"Where's Verulamium?"

"Oh, two or three days journey from here."

"Walking?"

"Goodness, no! With horses. We have a dozen horses. In fact, there's one of them over there." She pointed. A black stallion grazed in a circle around the stake it was tethered to. "My father had him brought over from Hispania. The horses here aren't as handsome as that." She spoke proudly.

"You must be very rich," Joe said.

"We are," she said, carelessly. "My father is very important. He goes to Rome quite often to report to the Emperor on the province. Of course, before he can do that, he has to travel round Britannia to see for himself what's going on. Sometimes, he's away for months at a time."

The way she was talking made Joe think of the kids in his class who boasted about their parents' business trips. "Do you miss him?" he asked.

She shrugged. "Not really. Even when he's here, he's so busy, we hardly see him."

Joe thought of his own dad. He was a history teacher and had seldom been away. Until now. For the first time, he decided to put Dad out of his mind. "I wish we were rich," he said instead.

"Mmmm." Lucy seemed not to be listening. "Let's sit down in the shade of that tree for a bit."

They crossed the grass together. "Now then, you know the first thing we need to do about you?"

Joe settled himself beside her, glad to get out of the sun again. "What's that?"

"We have to decide who we're going to say you are. People will ask, and it would be better to have an answer ready."

"I'm Joe Hopkins, I told you that."

She shook her head. "That won't do. It's not a very Latin name, is it? It sounds more like a Briton."

"That's because I am a Briton! Well, I'm British anyway, if that's the same thing."

"Well, in that case, you probably shouldn't be in the palace compound unless you're working, and that would mean you certainly shouldn't be talking to me. You don't want to pretend to work, do you?" She pulled a face. "You couldn't be part of my father's staff, so you'd have to be a slave. I'm sure you don't want to do that!"

Joe laughed. Then he realised she meant it. "A slave? Of course not! You have slaves?"

Lucy nodded. "Haven't you noticed them? Pretty much every person we've seen has been a slave. There's one weeding in the flower bed just by that bush." She pointed.

"One? Doesn't he have a name?"

"I don't know. It might be Privatus. Lots of the slaves are called Privatus."

"How many do you have, that you don't know their names?"

"Maybe a hundred, maybe a hundred and fifty. I honestly don't know." She picked a daisy and began to pull the petals off. "Anyway, as I was saying, we need to give you another name."

Joe watched her. One hundred and fifty slaves for a few rich people! That was outrageous! Yet Lucy clearly thought nothing of it.

"How about Titus Horatius Iovinus?" she said.

"Well, it's nothing like my real name," Joe said grumpily. "But since I don't speak Latin, it doesn't really matter. I won't be able to answer if anyone says anything to me."

"What on earth are you talking about? We're speaking Latin now!"

"We are?" Joe rubbed his forehead. He felt as though his brain hurt from adjusting to so many changes and surprises.

"I don't understand you at all!" Lucy was saying. "The questions you ask and the things you say! It's like you're from another world!"

"I think I am," Joe mumbled.

"Well that won't do as an explanation of who you are," she said firmly. "If someone asks, you're Titus Horatius Iovinus, which means that you'd be called Iovinus, or Joe for short." She grinned mischievously. "So now you are my cousin, the adopted son of my father's youngest brother."

Joe looked at her doubtfully.

"His family is due to arrive this afternoon," she continued, "along with both of my father's sisters' families. I thought you might be one of them when I found you in the north wing."

"But they'll know I'm not!"

"No, they won't. There will be lots of children for you to get yourself muddled with, and everyone will think you're with someone else. It's perfect!"

Joe groaned. Time travel was all very well in theory, but this was starting to sound like hard work. There was no way he would be able to pass himself off convincingly as a Roman. He'd already said quite a few things that Lucy clearly thought were either odd or stupid.

The trickiest thing of all was that he didn't feel at all sure of himself. He'd turned up in her time unexpectedly, to find himself wearing clothes that weren't his, and speaking a language that he knew he couldn't speak. And he hadn't even been aware of any of this happening. It was like finding yourself taking a test at school on a subject you'd never heard of.

"It's not perfect!" he said huffily. "It'll never work. The minute I open my mouth, they'll guess I'm a fake."

"Well, perhaps we should tell them you can't speak. That way, nobody can expect you to explain yourself."

Joe picked a blade of grass and split it with his thumb nail. "You're sure they'll be able to see me?" he asked. "Perhaps I might be invisible to everyone except you."

Lucy rolled her eyes. "That doesn't make any sense! Why would I be able to see you if no-one else can?"

Joe shrugged. "It was just a thought." And then he muttered, "After all, nothing else makes sense."

Lucy looked up at the sun. "Come on. It's nearly

time for dinner."

Joe looked at his watch, which of course wasn't there. "What time is it, then?"

"I'd say it's about half past three."

"As late as that?" Joe jumped to his feet. Butterflies whirled in his stomach.

"There's a sundial over there. We can check the time." Lucy got up and went over to a stone column that stood in the middle of the grass. "Yes, it's twenty to four. Dinner's at four, so we ought to go."

Joe looked over her shoulder at the symbols around the edge, hoping to read a different time. But he couldn't make out anything at all from it. "I really have to get back," he said. If Lucy was right, he was going to be in so much trouble with Mum. She'd said they would wait while he went to the loo, but that was almost three hours ago.

"Back where?"

"Back to where I came from."

"How are you going to do that?"

"I don't know." Joe's shoulders drooped. "I guess I'll go back to where you found me, and see what happens."

Lucy looked alarmed. "You can't go in there again! Although -" she thought for a moment. "If you're supposed to be from one of the guest families, that's where you'd be staying, so I guess that's alright."

"Let's go then!" Joe set off at a trot up the lawn towards the palace.

"If you do go back," Lucy said from behind him, "will you come again sometime?"

"I don't know." Worry made Joe snappy. "Let's see if I can get away first."

But as they reached the bath house, he realised there would be no chance of trying. Coming towards them along the eastern colonnade was a large group of people.

A woman with an elaborate decoration in her hair broke free from the front of the group. "There you are, Lucilia," she hissed. "We couldn't think where you'd got to!" Then, putting on a smile and a normal voice, "And this must be ...?"

"Titus Horatius Iovinus, Mother," said Lucy, bobbing in a kind of curtsey. "He's the adopted son of Tiberius Claudius." She ran forward a few steps to whisper in her mother's ear as the procession bore down on Joe.

"A mute!" exclaimed her mother. "How extraordinary!" She glanced over her shoulder at the people Joe supposed should be his parents. Fortunately, they were too far behind in the crowd for her to speak to them. "Well, bring him along with you, Lucilia."

Joe found himself shepherded along the colonnade of the south wing, and through a grand entrance into a hall overlooking the sea. Vast rugs were spread over the mosaic floors, and there were couches set in a circle around several low tables. At the foot of the couches, cushions were scattered across the floor.

"It's no good," Lucy whispered. "You'll have to eat with us first, and then see if you can get back later."

Joe felt his anxiety gathering inside him. "Couldn't I just slip out?" he whispered back, when Lucy's mother wasn't looking.

"No, not now that she's noticed you. Don't worry." She gestured to the low tables. "This is just going to be a normal meal, not a feast. It shouldn't take too long."

At that moment, two slaves appeared in front of them. Lucy took off her sandals, and nodded to Joe to do the same. The first slave set a large bowl on the floor, while the second knelt down with a jug and a towel. Joe looked at Lucy, who put her feet into the bowl, and allowed the slaves to wash and dry them. "They'll come round with clean water for washing our hands in a minute," she whispered, when they had washed Joe's feet and moved on.

Lucy's idea of not too long wasn't quite the same as his, Joe thought, as the sun slipped down the sky to the west. He wondered what time the museum closed. He felt as though there was a stopwatch running.

He sat beside Lucy on a cushion on the floor among the other children, while the adults reclined on the couches. Slaves wove in and out with platters of food, bringing quails' eggs and snails, spicy chicken and poached fish. They ate with their fingers, wiping them on the bread that accompanied each dish. Joe watched Lucy closely, eating what she ate and copying her movements exactly. He didn't dare speak to her or ask her anything, in case her mother saw him. It was strange to be completely silent among so much chatter. Lucy's mother, however, seemed to have forgotten the mute son of her brother-in-law, and was deep in conversation with one of the other women.

Fruit and cheese were brought, and then at last, the children were excused. Lucy drew Joe over to the corner, pointing out a small bronze statue to him. "Don't rush out," she murmured in his ear. "We need to look as though we're not in a hurry."

Joe glanced around. "It's okay for you!" he whispered back. "I've got to get away. Come on, let's go and look at that marble panel beside the door, and then make a run for it."

It was a warm evening outside, and in the formal gardens there wasn't a breath of wind.

"Thank God that's over!" Joe exploded with the relief of escape and of being able to speak normally again. "Do you actually like snails?"

She grinned. "Not much. But I knew you were copying me, and I wanted to see if you would eat them. They're a delicacy, you know, fattened on milk and blood!" Her eyes danced with merriment. Joe pretended to be sick.

"Come on then, if you're going."

They hurried round the east colonnade to the north wing, and through the first courtyard they came to. "If we go this way," she said under her breath, "we can see if there's anyone in any of the other rooms. You don't want to get caught."

But as they went along the corridor from the far end of the north wing, each room they passed was empty. The other courtyards were empty too. In the doorway of the room where Joe had arrived, he touched Lucy's arm. "Thanks for ..." he hesitated. "Thanks for having me, I suppose!" He grinned. "Who knows, maybe we'll meet again."

"You're not gone yet." She smiled. "But if you do get away, I'd be really happy if you came back." She gave him a little push into the room. "I'll just wait outside in the colonnade for a bit. Come and find me if you get stuck."

Joe stepped forward into the room that should have had the dolphin mosaic on the floor. He'd meant to ask her about that. There had been so many things he might have asked her. He went across the room to the sideboard and crouched down, as though he were looking for his St. Christopher again. He closed his eyes, lowered his head, and waited for something to happen.

3

Nothing did happen. Joe did his best to concentrate. He tried to picture this room as it had been in his own time, the absence of walls, the museum building like a barn over it, the dolphin mosaic. It was almost funny. Countless times, he had looked at a ruin and tried to imagine himself in the past when it had been a whole castle. Now, here he was, actually in the past, trying to imagine himself back to the present.

He crawled slowly along the length of the sideboard, thinking that he might as well look for his St. Christopher again while he waited. But he still couldn't find it.

After a few minutes, he stood up. He examined the space he had landed in earlier in the day, the floor, the air above it, even the ceiling. But there was nothing unusual about it, aside from the fact that he was standing in a time that wasn't his own. The novelty of that was wearing thin just at the moment.

He felt tired from the heat, and the strangeness of it all.

He walked about a little, and even jumped up and down a few times experimentally. At last, he went back out to the colonnade.

Lucy was sitting between two of the pillars, looking out at the gardens. At the sound of his footsteps, she turned. "You're still here!" Her face lit up. "I didn't come in, in case I put you off."

Joe shrugged. At least she was pleased. "I didn't know how to do it," he said.

"Never mind." She climbed back through the pillars. "We'll think of something."

"I suppose so." But Joe couldn't see how. "Shall we go and do something else?" He made himself speak more cheerfully than he felt. Since he couldn't do anything about getting back just at the moment, he supposed he ought to make the most of being here.

Lucy looked up at the sky again. "I'd guess it's coming up for eight o'clock. We could go down to the seashore before bedtime."

As they walked back around the formal garden, however, Joe realised that something else was bothering him. "Do you know where I can sleep?" he asked. "If I'm going to be staying here for a while, I'll need somewhere." The thought of his own bed at home crept into his mind. He pushed it away.

Lucy looked thoughtful. "The visitors will all be in the north wing," she said. "But you can't really stay there. There's one family in each suite of rooms, so you'd be noticed, whichever one we put you in."

"Can I stay somewhere not too far from you?"

"That's not easy," she said. "I could ask specially for you to come and stay in our residence. But I don't know if my mother would allow it. And then there's the whole thing about you not speaking at all."

Joe grinned ruefully. "You're right! I'm not sure I can keep quiet that long, even if I'm asleep half the time."

Lucy nudged a small stone along with her toe as she walked. "I know what we'll do." She stopped. "We'll ask Arethusa. She'll be able to help us."

"Who's that?"

"She's my slave. Well, ours. She's looked after me and my brothers and sisters since we were babies."

"Like a kind of nanny, you mean?"

"I don't know. What's a nanny?"

"Rich families have them. It's someone who looks after all the children."

"In that case, yes, I suppose so." Lucy flipped the stone with her toe. "In fact, let's go and find her now. It would be better to get it sorted out before everyone else comes to bed."

Joe and Lucy crept past the entrance to the south wing. The meal had been cleared away, and most people had gone out on to the terrace on the other side of the building, overlooking the sea. The sound of their voices carried on the still air, the adults talking and laughing, the children calling to one another in the gardens below.

"In here!" Lucy disappeared through a doorway at the end of the building. Joe followed.

The room they entered was dim and noisy. It was also roasting hot. Joe peered around. There were at least fifteen people in a very small space, and a fire glowed in an open oven. What seemed like hundreds of metal bowls, plates and goblets were being wiped with straw or bread, and then clattered into stacks on the stone work surfaces.

"Come on," Lucy called to him. "Ignore them. They're just clearing up. Arethusa will be down here somewhere."

She led the way along a corridor, glancing into the rooms they passed. Away from the room where they had entered the building, it was immediately quiet again.

"Is that where they cook the food?" Joe asked.

"Where? In that little room? Oh no! That's just where it's reheated and served. The kitchens are on the far side of the compound. Arethusa takes us over there sometimes, to watch what's going on, although we're not really allowed to go in there."

"Why not?"

"Because of the fires, I suppose, and the vats of boiling soup and stuff." She looked out through a doorway. "Here she is."

Joe followed Lucy into a small courtyard which

overlooked the terrace and then the gardens. A woman sat sewing beneath a vine.

"Are those grapes edible?" Joe eyed the bunches that hung among the leaves.

"Not for a few weeks. If you're still here in September, they'll be ripe then."

Joe gulped. Still here in September? Whenever he'd thought about time travel, he'd always assumed he would be able to come and go as he chose. It had never occurred to him that you might get stuck somewhere else permanently.

"Hello, Arethusa," Lucy said.

The woman put her sewing aside and stood up. "Miss Lucilia," she said, with a curtsey.

"Please, don't stop what you're doing, or not for a minute, anyway."

"Thank you, Miss." The woman sat down again.

Joe grinned to himself. Lucy had suddenly turned into a little princess. It was clear from her voice that she liked Arethusa, but she was obviously used to giving orders.

"This is my friend, Iovinus," Lucy said. "Though I just call him Joe."

Joe stepped forward. "Pleased to meet you, Arethusa." He held out his hand. Arethusa took it uncertainly.

Lucy shot him a look.

"What?" he said indignantly. "That's what we do, where I come from."

"Not with slaves," she hissed.

"We don't have slaves," he hissed back. "Slavery is evil."

"Anyway," Lucy flushed. She cleared her throat. "Joe is a visitor, but he's not with the other families that arrived today. Mother thinks he can't speak -"

"- because you told her I couldn't!" interrupted Joe.

"We decided that would be best, remember?" Lucy's eyes flashed. "As I was saying," she continued pointedly, "Mother thinks he can't speak, but that's quite difficult for him to keep up."

Arethusa put down her sewing. "What is it that you'd like me to do, Miss?"

"I'd like you to find him somewhere to sleep, not too far from me if that's possible, but where no-one is likely to find him. Nobody must know he's here, do you understand? That's really important."

Arethusa shook her head and smiled. "You are a one, Miss Lucilia. Whatever are you going to ask next?"

"You won't tell anyonc, will you?"

"Of course not, Miss. You know you can trust me."

"Thank you!" Lucy looked suddenly relieved. "Thank you so much, Arethusa."

Joe wondered if her imperiousness had been put on for his benefit. She sounded so much more friendly now.

"Let's see." Arethusa stood up again. "Where could we put you?" She thought for a minute. "Much better if no-one but me knows you're here, so you can't sleep anywhere that the other slaves go. If you don't mind being shut in, there's a closet we could use."

Joe nodded.

"I can fetch you a mattress and make you up a bed on the floor. It might not be the most comfortable place, but I'm the only person who ever goes in there, and it would do for tonight."

"That's very kind of you," Joe said.

"You haven't seen it yet, Master Joe!" Arethusa smiled. "Why don't you two go off and amuse yourselves? Come back here in half an hour."

"You're wonderful, Arethusa! Thank you!" Lucy danced out on to the terrace and jumped down on to the lawn beneath. "Shall we go down to the beach?" she called to Joe.

"Actually -" He felt his cheeks turn red. "Before we do, is there a toilet somewhere?"

"It's fine to pee in the bushes. Almost everyone does that here."

Joe ran to catch her up. "I need more than a pee," he muttered.

Lucy laughed. "You can do that in the bushes too. Plenty do."

"Really?" Joe pulled a face. "That's a bit gross, isn't it?"

"Gross?"

"Nasty, I mean. Unhygienic. Isn't there somewhere proper to go, with so many people living here?"

She stood still. "There is. Do you really want me to take you all the way up there? It's behind the bath house."

"Yes, please." Joe dug his toe into the grass. She probably thought he was being pathetic, but he didn't want to get caught wandering around without her. Goodness knows what might happen.

"I don't know why you're being so fussy!" Lucy stumped back up the lawn.

They went back round the western end of the south wing, and along the side of the formal gardens once more. From the main hall came the sound of singing and someone strumming on what sounded to Joe like some kind of guitar.

"It's over there." Lucy pointed to a long low building in the south eastern corner of the compound. "It's communal, so if anyone comes in, remember that you can't speak!"

Hesitantly, Joe went over to the building. Without Lucy beside him, he felt exposed and vulnerable. He glanced over his shoulder, but she was looking the other way. There was no-one else to be seen.

Inside the building, it was much less dark than Joe had expected. The roofs which stretched out from either side didn't meet in the middle, so you could see the sky. They sloped in the opposite direction from the usual way, too, making a shape which would have been a 'V' if they had joined.

Along the two long walls were raised benches, and down the middle of the floor was a long trough flowing with water. Every couple of metres, there was a large container with a bundle of sticks standing in it, like the handles of giant paintbrushes left in giant jars. Joe looked around and wondered what to do. He should have asked Lucy to explain before he came in. But it seemed so stupid, having to ask for help to go to the loo.

He walked down to the far end of the building and climbed the step to one of the raised benches. There was a large, round hole every metre or so along the bench that he hadn't been able to see from the floor. That made it much more obvious, he thought with relief.

He pulled down the linen shorts he seemed to be wearing under his tunic, and sat down over one of the holes. The use of the sticks and water was still unclear. He waited quietly to see if someone else would come in and show him.

After a minute or so, a man appeared in the doorway and came and sat down half way along the opposite wall. Seeing Joe, he raised his hand. "Ave."

Joe raised his hand and nodded, but said nothing, conscious of Lucy's reminder. He watched the man covertly, to see whether he would use the sticks or the water. Sure enough, the man leaned forward and took a stick from the container nearest him. On the end of it was a piece of sponge. The man dipped this into the water, shook it, wiped his backside with it, rinsed it in the water once more, and put it back in the container.

Joe gaped.

The man stood up and pulled up his underclothes. "Vale," he said, and left.

Joe leaned over to the container in front of him and picked out the cleanest looking stick. The sponge attached to it was still dripping with water from the bottom of the container. It didn't look too clean. He put it back and tried another, and then another.

Finally, when he had examined and rejected every single one, he picked a stick at random, waggled the sponge hard in the water trough, and used it to clean himself. His stomach turned at the thought of using something that so many other people had already used before him. Perhaps a bush wasn't such a bad thing after all. At least the leaf you used would be your own.

"There you are!" Lucy exclaimed as he emerged. "I was starting to think you'd fallen in."

Joe laughed sheepishly.

"It does happen, you know," she said, without a flicker of a smile. "People drown. Not a nice way to die!"

"My God! No!" Horror gripped Joe's throat.

"Let's go, shall we?" He hurried ahead of her back along the side of the bath house, keen to get as far away as he could.

"We haven't got long now," Lucy called, running to catch up with him. "Arethusa said half an hour, so we'll have to go back in about ten minutes. Shall we go to the orchard?"

Joe slowed down. "Okay."

"What *does* that mean? You keep saying it."

"What? 'Okay'? It means 'alright', 'I agree'."

"I see. Okay," Lucy said. She grinned. "I sound like you!"

"Do you?"

"Well, a bit. It's like you're from a different part of the empire - you're talking away completely normally, and then out pops a word that either isn't Latin or doesn't fit. You used another one earlier. What was it?" She furrowed her brow in thought. "That's it, 'gross'. We have that word, but not the way you used it."

"Oh." Joe didn't know what to say. He still found it hard to believe that he and Lucy were speaking Latin together.

"Here we are," she said now.

"This is the orchard?" Joe was faintly disappointed. He had imagined big, gnarled apple trees that you could climb. But these were just saplings, planted in strict rows.

"What did you expect?"

"I don't know. Something older, I suppose."

"But I told you already, the whole palace was only finished last year. That's when these were planted." She walked along one of the rows. "They're doing well, actually. Look at the fruit on this one."

"What is that?"

"It's a medlar. Haven't you seen one before? I'd pick one for you to try, but they're not ripe yet, so they won't taste good. There are apples and pears and quinces too. And oranges and lemons over there on the wall."

"Oh, yes." Joe sat down on the grass at the end of one of the rows. Despite the novelty of it, he couldn't get excited about oranges and lemons growing in England. The tiredness he'd felt earlier had returned, and with it, a sense of gloom. He longed for his own bed in his own room, at home with Mum and Sam. They must have given up waiting for him and left the museum long ago. He wondered whether the police had been called, and whether they were treating his disappearance as suspicious. He felt bad for the worry he must be causing.

"Let's go back," Lucy said, noticing the change in his mood. "Arethusa has probably got everything ready by now, and everyone else will start coming to bed as it gets dark, so it would be better if you were hidden away by then."

Joe followed her, back along the south wing and through the room at the end, now empty of people.

In the courtyard, Arethusa stood up at once. "Everything's ready for your friend, Miss Lucilia." She led the way down a narrow passageway between two rooms, to a tiny room at the back. The mattress she had put down on the floor took up all of the available space. Racks of linen towered over it on three sides.

"Thank you, Arethusa. This is perfect!" Lucy said.

"Yes, thank you." Joe sank down on the end of the mattress. It felt lumpy.

"There's a nightshirt for Master Joe," Arethusa said, "and some toothpaste and a toothcloth by the oil lamp there."

Joe looked around. "Toothpaste?"

"In that little pot with the lid." Lucy pointed. "You use the cloth to rub it on your teeth."

Joe took off the lid and looked inside. The paste was a very pale yellow and smelled of something familiar. "What's in it?"

Arethusa looked at Lucy, as though for permission to answer. "It's the usual recipe, Master Joe. The ashes of dogs' bones mixed with honey."

Joe put the lid back on hastily. "Thank you very much, Arethusa." He looked up at Lucy. "I think I might go to sleep if that's okay - I mean if that's alright? It's been a really strange day and I'm exhausted."

Lucy smiled. "Arethusa will wake you in the morning, won't you, Arethusa?"

The slave nodded.

"Goodnight, Joe. May the good spirits watch over you and keep you safe."

The door closed behind them. Joe pulled off his tunic and put on the nightshirt. He blew out the oil lamp and lay down in the darkness. What would Dad make of all this, he wondered ... and within seconds, he was fast asleep.

4

He was woken the next morning by a quiet tap on the door.

"Only me, Master Joe," Arethusa murmured. "I've brought you some breakfast. I thought Miss Lucilia's family might not be expecting you."

Joe sat up and rubbed his eyes, wondering for a moment where on earth he was. "Thank you very much," he said dazedly. "What's the time?"

"Half past five."

"Ugh." He yawned. "Is everyone else getting up?"

"Of course. It's past sunrise." Arethusa shook her head at him and gave him the tray. On it were a metal cup filled with water and a large metal plate of bread and fruit.

Joe shifted to get comfortable. The lumps in the mattress he'd noticed last night had clumped together, leaving some bits completely empty, and it felt itchy through the cover. It was amazing that he'd slept so deeply. He frowned.

"What's the matter, Master Joe?" Arethusa was instantly anxious.

"Nothing. I think I'm half sitting on the floor, that's all."

"I can shake the mattress for you, if you stand up."

"No, don't worry. What's in it, though? It smells funny."

Arethusa looked at him. "The same as always."

"But what's that?"

"Wool, straw, and feathers." She shook her head again and went out.

Joe wondered what she thought of him. He put the tray down and folded the mattress over on itself, then sat down again and rested the plate on his knees.

The bread was heavy and dark. He chewed his way dutifully through about half of it, and then gave up and started on the fruit. There were apricots and plums, raspberries and figs, and pieces of melon and strawberries too, all of it ripe and delicious. By the time he'd eaten as much as he could, the idea of staying here a while longer didn't seem nearly as bad as it had done last night.

He took off his nightshirt and put on the tunic and belt he'd worn yesterday. At some point, he supposed, he would need some clean clothes, but he didn't need to worry about that just yet. At home, he would usually have a wash and clean his teeth too, but he didn't fancy the toothpaste, and there was no-one to make him do it. He gave a quiet whoop in his linen closet. What freedom!

He had put the mattress flat once more and was wondering what to do about meeting Lucy when there was another tap on the door.

"Excuse me disturbing you again, Master Joe. Miss Lucilia says you're to meet her in the informal gardens, by the tree where you sat yesterday. She said you'd know which one."

"Thank you, Arethusa. And thank you for the breakfast!" Joe beamed at her.

Her eyes fell on the bread and the last of the fruit.

"Would you like that?" he asked. "There was too much for me. That's the only reason I didn't finish it."

Arethusa blushed. "I wouldn't want you to think ..."

"Please eat it. Nobody will know."

She smiled shyly. "Thank you, Master Joe."

Lucy was waiting for him when he got to the tree she had suggested. "What took you so long? I was starting to worry."

"I came the long way round. I didn't want to bump into anyone."

Like him, she was wearing the same clothes as yesterday, but her hair was wound up and pinned with combs decorated with pearly white shell. She was very pretty, he thought. He'd been too taken up with everything else yesterday to notice.

"Shall we go down to the seashore, then?" she said. "I've got lessons this morning, but there's still time."

Together they walked down the sloping lawns in the early morning sunshine.

"What are you learning about?" Joe asked.

"Nothing very interesting. My sisters and I do reading and writing exercises and some arithmetic. And today we're doing weaving."

"That sounds like fun."

She wrinkled her nose. "Not really. You do the same thing over and over, so you soon get bored."

"What are you making?"

"Nothing yet. Antonia and I are still just practising. Later on, we'll make drapes, I suppose, like Sallustia, or material for clothes maybe, if we get good. Sallustia's not bad. She's working really hard at it. But that's because she has to, if she's going to be ready in time."

"In time for what?"

"Getting married."

Joe frowned. "How old did you say she was?"

"Thirteen."

"So when's she going to be married?"

"Any time. It hasn't been arranged yet, but it won't be long."

He stopped walking and stared at her. "That's awful!"

Lucy laughed. "No, it's not! It's normal. She could have got married last year. She's old enough."

"Does she want to?"

"I don't know." She looked at him curiously. "That's just how things are. We don't really talk about it."

They reached the water. There was no beach, just a broad shingle edge creeping out beneath the grass.

"What about boys?" Joe asked. "Do they get married that young?"

"I think they can get married at fourteen, but they're usually a bit older. Marius is sixteen and Tiberius is fifteen, but I don't think there are plans for either of them at the moment." She picked up a stone and skimmed it across the surface of the water.

"Who are Marius and Tiberius? I thought you only had sisters!"

"Marius is my eldest brother, and Tiberius is adopted."

"Why did your parents adopt when they had your brother already?"

"They had five of us when they adopted Tiberius. He's my father's nephew. He came to live with us after his father died and his mother remarried."

"Hang on. Let me get this straight: there's Marius, then Tiberius, then Sallustia, then you, then Antonia."

"And Petrus. He's twelve, so he's between me

and Sallustia. There was Flavius as well, but he died."

"When was that?"

Lucy picked up another stone. It bounced six times on the water. "Two years ago, before we came here. He was the littlest, only four."

"That's really sad," Joe said.

Lucy shrugged.

"Didn't you mind?"

"Of course I did! I loved him! He used to come everywhere with me. They said he was my doll. That's why they gave his bulla to me, not to Sallustia." She tugged at the pendant around her neck. "Not that it worked! It's meant to keep away evil spirits, but they still got him." She picked up a rock and hurled it into the water. "I suppose it's just what happens sometimes."

Joe didn't know what to say. He picked up a stone and skimmed it over the sea.

"That was a good one," Lucy said.

Joe tried to think of a way of changing the subject. He didn't want to think about Lucy's little brother dying, and it seemed like she didn't want to think about it either. But he didn't want to seem uncaring.

"What's that over there?" He pointed to a dark smudge on the horizon.

Lucy looked up. "It's a ship!" She clapped her hands. "How exciting! I love it when a ship comes in!"

"Will it land here?"

"No. There's a quay further along."

Joe looked where she indicated. "Shall we go down there to meet it?" he suggested.

"No point yet. It'll be another couple of hours before it's in. We'll go after my lessons."

"What's on it?"

"Who knows? Could be food, or cloth. Or building materials. Or even animals. That's what I love. It's always a surprise." She looked up at the sun. "I should probably go. I'll be in trouble if I'm late. Shall we meet down here later?"

"Okay - I mean, alright." He grinned. "I'll never speak good Latin!"

"It's fine. I like it!"

"So, what time then?"

"Just after ten o'clock. My lessons are from seven till ten at this time of year."

"And how will I know when it's ten o'clock?"

She smiled. "The sun will be about there." She pointed at the sky.

"Right." Joe frowned. "Let's hope I can remember that."

He watched her hurry away up the long lawn to the palace and wondered what it would be like to stay here always. Quite suddenly, he felt a rush of homesickness so strong, he thought he might actually throw up. He sat down on the grass and put his head on his knees. It wouldn't happen! It couldn't happen! Because if he was here forever, he would have to become part of all this. He shivered. There seemed to be a lot of things that were either uncomfortable or downright horrible, even when you were rich like Lucy's family. He couldn't bear to think about it.

When the sickness had gone, he got up and began to walk along the shore towards the quay, trying to decide how to pass the time until Lucy came back. Perhaps he should go up to the other side of the palace and see where the slaves lived, he thought. That would be the flip-side to Lucy's life. He felt a spark of curiosity. She was so offhand about them, but he was willing to bet that she knew next to nothing about how they lived.

The more he thought about it, the more it seemed like a good way of spending the time. It would be the kind of thing they would do on a school trip, and he felt comforted by the idea. It made being here seem more normal. In any case, Lucy probably wouldn't be allowed to visit the slave quarters, and she certainly wouldn't be able to slip through, unseen. That was one aspect of her life that wasn't so different from his own - there were lots of things she wasn't allowed to do and places she wasn't allowed to go. Grown-ups always said that children had had more freedom in the past. But maybe that wasn't strictly true.

He kept to the edge of the gardens, hurrying from one shrub to the next just in case anyone was looking out from the south wing. If he got caught by Lucy's mother, it could be a disaster. For all he knew, she might already have remarked to her sister-in-law about adopting a mute boy. Certainly, as soon as she did, the game would be up. He refused to let himself imagine what punishment might follow.

When he reached the palace buildings, he stopped at the end of the south wing. The colonnades were busy now, where yesterday they had been mostly deserted.

A few feet away, a man squatted, carving a large piece of wood. Further along, two men were hoisting the trunk of a tree on to a saw horse, and beyond that, some women sat and sewed. Around all four colonnades, individuals and small groups of people were busy with different activities.

Others scurried from one part of the palace to another, carrying all manner of things - an armful of what looked like scrolls, a pair of leather buckets, various sorts of gardening tools, piles of linen, pots and dishes, baskets of fruit and wool.

Joe watched, fascinated. Nobody went into the formal gardens, except for a gardener who moved along the paths, clipping the short, thick hedges.

It was so much like watching a film that he forgot that he was a visible part of the scene. So he jumped, startled, to find someone close beside him.

"Never seen people working before?" The boy who'd spoken was a few years older than him and quite a bit taller.

"Yes, but not like this," Joe said, truthfully.

"Oh dear," the boy drawled. "Another one awed by the glories of Fishbourne. It's very boring, how impressed everyone is when they come here."

Joe looked up at him. He had curly, black hair and broad shoulders. He should have been handsome, but his mouth was turned down at the corners giving him a sour expression.

"Whose son are you?" the boy asked.

Too late, Joe remembered that he wasn't supposed to be able to speak. This was exactly the situation he'd hoped to avoid. He tried desperately to remember who Lucy had said he should pretend to be.

"What's the matter with you?" The boy narrowed his eyes. "Cat got your tongue?"

"Claudius Maximus Antonius," Joe babbled, stringing together the only Latin-sounding names he could think of.

"Claudius Maximus Antonius?" The boy laughed nastily. "Do you want to try again?"

Joe shook his head dumbly.

"Because all our visitors are family, and those names don't belong to any of us. In fact, what you've just come out with isn't a normal name at all!"

Joe looked at his feet and said nothing.

"Claudius always comes second, you see. It's a *nomen*, not a *praenomen*." The boy took a step closer to Joe. "There's something funny about you, isn't there? I thought so from the way you were watching everyone. Who are you really?"

"I'm nobody," Joe muttered to the ground.

The boy cuffed him on the shoulder. "It's polite to look at someone when they speak to you."

Still Joe couldn't bring himself to raise his eyes above the boy's knees. He felt a hand catch him roughly under the chin, forcing his head up.

"There! That's better, don't you think? Now I'm going to ask you again. Who are you?" The boy bared his teeth.

Joe made himself look into the boy's eyes. They glittered. Joe blinked. The expression in them was as close to evil as he had ever seen. He looked away.

"Well?" snapped the boy.

Joe opened his mouth to answer, but no words came out. He winced, sure that the boy was going to hit him. He didn't dare look.

All at once, his surroundings dwindled away. The air hissed. He swayed and blinked. The boy had vanished. The palace had vanished too, and with it, all the people. Joe stood on the dolphin mosaic, wearing his own clothes, in his own time.

He scrambled up through the rail on to the walkway and looked around. There was nobody nearby. He closed his eyes and opened them again. He was definitely back in the present.

Outside the windows of the museum, it was broad daylight and cloudy, just as it had been on the day he came here. He looked at his watch. One o'clock. Was it possible that no time had passed here at all? His heart leapt. He dashed back through the museum and out to the picnic area. There at the bench were his mum and Kate, with Sam and Ben.

"Are you alright, Joe?" His mum sounded concerned. "What's the big hurry? You didn't think we'd go without you, did you?"

Joe shook his head and tried to catch his breath. "Nothing, it's fine. I mean, I'm okay." He smiled at her.

"I'm glad you've cheered up, anyway. Did someone find your St. Christopher for you?"

"What?" He looked at her blankly. "Oh, no. No sign of it." He hoped she wouldn't notice his confusion.

His mum looked at Kate. "Sometimes these kids are a mystery, aren't they?"

Kate smiled. "Come and sit down again, Joe. Did you want your apple?"

Joe sank his teeth into it, grateful for something to anchor him in his own time again. It tasted real, and normal, just like an apple always tasted. He ate it in silence while everyone else talked on around him.

But at the back of his mind, he couldn't help wondering what an apple would taste like in Lucy's time.

5

Over the next two weeks, Joe found himself thinking constantly about Lucy and the palace. He went to the library and borrowed all the books he could find about Romans. A lot of them were about the army, which didn't really interest him, but there were a few about life in Roman times, and even one about Roman Britain.

It was odd, looking at pictures of the kind of place that was now familiar, a bit like looking at brochures for somewhere you'd been to. It seemed suddenly much more interesting too than it had done before, when he'd done a project at school about it.

"Fishbourne really caught your imagination, didn't it?" said Mum, finding him looking on the internet for information about it. "Funny, I didn't think you were all that keen the day we went." She seemed pleased.

"You know I like history," Joe said.

With all this to keep him busy, the time passed

quite quickly until he and Sam were due to stay with Dad. Joe was still looking forward to it, but he'd stopped counting the days. When he lay in bed at night, it was Lucy's life he thought about.

It was daft - while he'd been with her, he'd spent half the time worrying about how to get home. But now that he was safe in his own time, he found himself wondering over and over whether he could get back to Lucy's time again. Knowing that nobody here would even notice he'd gone, he felt he would enjoy himself more, if only he could find a way of getting there.

Mum fussed around while he and Sam packed their stuff for the trip to Dad's. "I know it doesn't matter if you forget something," she kept saying. "You could always call by and pick it up. I should leave you to it."

But she still insisted on checking their cases when they'd finished. "Do you really want to take all these library books, Joe?"

"Yes, Mum."

"Don't forget to bring them all home, then." She gave him a quick hug. "You're turning into your dad, you know, with this history obsession." She smiled, but he noticed her eyes were sad.

Dad seemed a bit tense too, when he picked them up the next morning. But once they were in the car, he chatted and laughed a lot. Joe thought perhaps he was happier now he'd moved out. He'd been getting cross with Joe almost every day when he was still living at home. And then he and Mum had called Joe and Sam into the kitchen and given them The Talk.

Joe had tried to wipe that from his memory, but he couldn't forget it. And even with everything they'd said, he still worried that maybe Dad had left because he'd annoyed him once too often.

Since then, they'd seen Dad a few times at weekends. It had been a bit awkward, because Dad hadn't had his own place, so they'd had to stay out all day. Now, he had a flat, so they could stay for a whole week. Joe looked out of the car window as they parked behind the building, and made up his mind to be as nice as he possibly could, so that Dad would be happy.

"This is it, then," Dad said. He entered the code on the keypad and pushed the door open. The stairwell was dark and smelled of rubbish. "Third floor, I'm afraid." He set off up the stairs ahead of them carrying both of their suitcases. "We'll get plenty of exercise over the next few days, coming and going!"

The flat was very small, just two rooms and a little kitchen area.

"We'll muddle along okay, won't we, boys?" Dad said in that bright voice that Mum used.

"It's nice," Joe fibbed.

Dad beamed.

Over breakfast the next morning, he said, "Is there anything particular you want to do this week? We could go swimming or bowling, we can see if there's anything on at the cinema, maybe even go for a day at the beach. But if there's something special either of you would really like to do, we can make sure we fit it in."

"I'd like to go to Fishbourne Roman Palace," Joe said.

Dad looked pleased, but Sam groaned. "Not again! We've only just been there, and there was nothing for kids!"

"We haven't been there with Dad," Joe said, stubbornly.

"I saw all the books you've been reading." Dad grinned. "Looks like you've been bitten by the history bug!"

"Just Romans," Joe said.

"Just Romans at the moment. We all start somewhere. Anyway, it's great that you like it! We'll go to Fishbourne on Wednesday then, shall we? It'll be my challenge to try and find something to interest Sam this time."

Joe woke up very early on Wednesday morning with his insides fluttering. He really did want to go to the palace again because he had a quite a few questions he wanted to ask. But he also hoped that he might find a way of getting back to see Lucy. Surely it would be possible somehow. It felt a bit disloyal, to be planning to leave Dad and Sam, as though he was thinking of running away. But they wouldn't know anything about it, so it wouldn't hurt them.

Sam was grumpy all the way there. He didn't say much, but he'd complained so noisily the evening before that Dad had let him download Angry Birds on to his phone. He sat in the back of the car, his eyes glued to the screen, while the phone chirruped annoyingly beside Joe.

"Can we see the film?" Joe asked, when they got there.

"Why do you want to watch it again?" Sam glowered.

"Dad hasn't seen it," said Joe. "And anyway, I thought it was interesting."

This time, it was Sam who sat on the end of the row with his shoulders hunched because Dad had said he had to give the phone back for a bit. "It's not fair," he huffed. "This is so boring."

But Joe could barely contain his excitement. "Look at that!" He pointed at the screen as the computer graphics conjured the palace from its ruins. "That's exactly how it was. I mean -" He bit his lip. "That's how it must have been." He was going to have to be much more careful.

Dad beamed at his enthusiasm.

Joe watched the film a lot more closely than last time. The general impression was exactly right, even if the detail was a bit blurry. It reminded him of the drawings you saw around building sites, of what the new buildings were going to look like, with trees around and people walking past. They never looked exactly like that when they were finished, but the idea was there.

There was one big thing they had got wrong, though, he was sure of it. "Who did they say it was built for?" he asked Dad, when they came out of the auditorium.

"King Togidubnus, I think. Here," Dad flicked through the leaflet he'd picked up. "There it is: Togidubnus or Cogidubnus - there are different spellings, but it's the same person."

Joe frowned. He couldn't remember what Lucy had said her father's name was, but it wasn't that, and he definitely hadn't been a king. "Do they know that for certain?"

"Probably not," Dad said. "The evidence left from Roman times is usually pretty sketchy, so archaeologists have to guess a lot of it."

"But they've got so much of the rest right!"

Dad smiled again. "We presume so. But there's no way of knowing, is there?"

Joe looked away. It was so hard not to say something.

"Shall we have a look around together, and then take the guided tour in half an hour?"

"Do we have to?" Joe's brother was still sulking.

"Come on, Sam. Cheer up!" Dad consulted his plan of the palace. "Let's go and have a look in the physic garden and see what bizarre herbal remedies they used for medicine. I'm ready to bet that some of their concoctions were pretty nasty."

"Like toothpaste made with the ashes of dogs' bones!" Joe said.

Dad laughed. "Did they really do that? You've probably picked up more than I can tell you from all those books you've read."

While they waited for the tour, they wandered around the gardens and the small orchard. It wasn't the same orchard that Lucy had shown to Joe. For one thing, it was in completely the wrong place. Where those trees had grown, there were now houses and roads. There weren't any orange or lemon trees either. Joe supposed it wasn't warm enough in England any more. It had been much hotter in Lucy's time than it ever was now.

From over the fence, he could hear the noise of passing traffic. That was another thing. It had been really quiet in Lucy's time. He hadn't thought about it till now. He felt a bit sad. There was almost nothing left of the wonderful place he had seen, and he would have so loved to share it with Dad.

While Dad spun his stories around everything they looked at, Joe found for the first time that he was listening to them critically, comparing what Dad was dreaming up with how he knew it had been.

They joined the start of the guided tour at the model of the palace in the foyer.

"First of all," said the guide, "let me explain what each part of the palace might have been used for.

You have to remember that we're not certain about a lot of this, and that it changed over the two hundred years that the palace was in use."

Joe shuffled to get closer to the model.

"We're standing here at the end of the north wing-" The guide pointed. "The mosaics you can see over there are the remaining floors. We think this wing might have been three suites of rooms for important visitors, though it's possible that a second family lived here permanently."

Joe frowned. There hadn't been a second family living in the palace in Lucy's time. But rooms for visitors would be right.

"Over here," the guide pointed to another area on the model, "is the west wing, built at a higher level than the rest of the palace. From the floors we found, we believe these were also important rooms, perhaps for state functions such as an audience with King Cogidubnus, or possibly the living area of the king and his close family."

Joe shook his head. That definitely wasn't right. Lucy's family lived in the south wing. And he was sure her father wasn't King Cogidubnus.

"Is something confusing you, young man?"

Joe looked up. The guide was talking to him.

"No, sorry." He felt himself turn red.

Fortunately, the guide didn't seem put out. "We know almost nothing about the south wing, because houses were built over that area long before the site was discovered. However, we do know the general layout from excavations in some of the back gardens, and we think there may also have been an informal garden with a stream and a pond."

Joe kept his face carefully neutral. He would go and look for the pond if he did manage to get back to Lucy's time again.

"And finally, the east wing. We think this had the entrance hall in the middle, possibly with a fountain in the centre, and with offices or other administrative areas to either side. You should remember, this was the home of somebody of great political importance, when it was first built, at least."

Joe put up his hand. "Where are the buildings where the slaves lived on this model?"

The guide looked up. "That's a very good question. They're not on here, because we've never found them. We've excavated all of the site you can see today, but we haven't found any trace of the slave quarters, or the kitchens, or any other outbuildings."

Joe scratched his head. He was sure the kitchens and the slaves' accommodation had been on the north side of the compound. But why had nothing been found? He wondered if he was wrong. That was what Lucy had said, he was certain.

"We'll move to the mosaics now," said the guide.

Joe and his dad followed with the rest of the group. Sam had sat down on a bench and was playing Angry Birds again. Joe felt a prick of guilt at having made his brother put up with this.

"In this room here," said the guide, "we can see the exposed workings of a hypocaust, the Roman equivalent of central heating. If this had been finished, a floor would have been laid on top of the stacks of tiles to be heated by warm air beneath. But it was still being built when the palace burned down."

"Burned down?" The words were out of Joe's mouth before he could stop them. How had he missed this before? "When?"

"In about 270 or 280." The guide smiled. "Still a very long time ago. There's no need to be upset about it."

Joe blushed again. He tried to work out when Lucy had lived here. "When was the palace built?"

"The version in the model was probably built in about AD80, though there was another smaller villa on this site before that."

But Joe's brain was already whirring. If the palace was built in AD80, Lucy must have lived here in about AD82. So by the year 270, she would have been - he struggled with the arithmetic for a moment - almost 200 years old. He almost laughed at his own foolishness. It was the same as worrying about a child living in 1820 being caught in a fire today. At the same time, it was strange to think of a girl his own age growing old and dying, hundreds and hundreds of years ago.

"Moving on to the room next door," the guide was saying, "we see the famous mosaic of cupid riding a dolphin."

Joe gazed down. He was standing just a couple of metres away from where he had landed in Lucy's time, on a black and white floor nothing like this one. He stared at the circles and curls of coloured tiles. Was it possible he was mistaken about this too? He couldn't believe he had imagined the zigzag design, even if the lack of colour had been a trick of the light. But the dolphin mosaic had clearly been here for centuries.

He put up his hand again.

"Is this the room where this mosaic was put down originally?"

"It is." The guide smiled. "As you can imagine, once you put down tens or even hundreds of thousands of tiles, you don't just move them on a whim!" He gave a little laugh. "We discovered this for ourselves, in fact, when we removed a section of the mosaic to try to date it. Underneath was another mosaic, a black and white one that you can now see down at the far end of the museum hall."

Joe clasped his hands tightly together. He hadn't been wrong, after all!

"We had to take all of this up," the guide was saying, "then we lifted the black and white mosaic beneath, before relaying this mosaic again afterwards."

Joe couldn't contain himself. "So the dolphin mosaic wasn't here when the palace was built?"

"That's right. At that time, the black and white mosaic was in this room and those two large outer rooms nearest the gardens were courtyards, because it was much warmer and wetter than it is now. Then, eighty or ninety years later, new owners had this mosaic put down, rather as you might have new carpets. They made lots of other changes to the palace too, including building hypocausts, probably because the weather had got colder by then."

Joe was still digesting this information as they continued around the other mosaics. It hadn't seemed at all important to know this sort of thing when he was with Lucy, but it mattered to him now. If he was going to try to get back to her, he wanted to know as much as possible.

"Does anyone have any further questions?" the guide asked at the end of the tour. The rest of the group shook their heads and melted away, until only Joe and his dad were left.

"Actually, there was one other thing," Joe said.

"Goodness me!" the guide said. "I wish all the children I showed round were as interested as you. Fire away!"

"You said the palace was built for a king."

"That's right. King Cogidubnus. That's the most popular theory. Unfortunately, there's not much evidence either way."

"So it could have been built for someone else?"

The guide looked surprised. "Yes, it's certainly possible. In fact, there's quite a convincing argument that it might have been built for the man who was the governor of this province around that time, Gaius

Sallustius Lucullus."

Joe bit down hard on his tongue to stop himself from saying anything. That was definitely him! That was Lucy's father. He repeated the name in his head to try to remember it.

"If you're really interested, there's a good book I can recommend to you."

Joe looked up at his dad.

"Would you like it?" asked Dad.

"Yes, please!"

"I must admit, it's not written for children," the guide said, as he led the way back to the museum shop. "They usually go for 'Rotten Romans'. Still, I think this young man might enjoy it."

He gave the book to Joe's dad and disappeared off. Joe looked around. He did want the book, but he also wanted to try and get back to Lucy. There hadn't been a moment so far.

While Dad waited at the till to pay, Joe seized his chance.

"I must just go to the loo," he said. "I'll be back in a minute." Or in several hours, or days, if I can manage it, he added silently.

He hurried towards the mosaics again, glancing over his shoulder to make sure Dad wasn't looking. His luck seemed to hold, because again there was nobody looking at the dolphin mosaic.

For a second time, he climbed quickly through the rail, and dropped down onto the floor below.

6

"What on earth do you think you're doing?"

Joe froze. He could hear Dad's footsteps hurrying along the walkway towards him.

"I thought you said you were going to the loo!"

Joe stared at his feet on the coloured tiles of the mosaic. He was sure this was exactly the place he'd climbed down last time. But it hadn't worked. He was still here, in the present. And now he was going to be in trouble.

"He's probably looking for his St. Christopher," Sam called out.

Joe climbed back up through the rail.

"The one I gave you?" Dad stopped in front of him. "Oh, Joe."

Joe hung his head and said nothing.

"He dropped it down there last time we were here. I bet that's why he really wanted to come again." Sam was smug.

"It's not!" Joe was about to add that he'd

forgotten all about it, but one look at Dad's face stopped him. He swallowed.

"How did you lose it?" Dad asked quietly.

"The chain broke, and it fell down and rolled away. The guide last time looked for it, but he couldn't find it." Joe felt tears prickling at the back of his eyes.

"Even so," Dad said. "You know you shouldn't have climbed down on to the mosaic. Imagine if everybody walked on it." He sighed. "Never mind. I expect it'll be okay. And it's too bad about the St. Christopher." He handed Joe the book he'd just bought for him. "Take better care of this, please. Now, shall we look around the rest of the museum quickly? I think Sam has suffered long enough, so we'll go soon."

Joe followed his dad around the information boards and exhibit cases, trying to pretend that he was interested. But his heart wasn't in it any more. What was the point in learning anything else about the place if he couldn't get back into Lucy's time again? He'd been so sure he would manage it somehow.

As they drove into Chichester to have lunch, Sam chattered non-stop, clearly feeling that he was now in favour. Joe stared out of the window, too miserable to care. They had so little time with Dad. Why had he gone and spoiled today?

That evening, he tossed and turned in bed, unable to get to sleep. Sam snored beside him. It was alright for him, Joe thought bitterly. He pulled the pillow over his head to try and block out the noise and muffle the thoughts that churned in his brain. He needed something else to think about. But the only thing he ever thought about these days was Lucy's world. And Lucy had been the cause of all this trouble in the first place.

Beneath the pillow, he felt as though the room moved around him. There was a hissing sound in his ears. He lifted the pillow, thinking that perhaps he was dizzy from lack of air. But he found his hands were empty.

It was broad daylight, sunny and bright. He blinked. He was no longer lying down but standing up. And he wasn't in Dad's flat, but back at the palace, at the south-west corner of the colonnades, exactly where he'd been when he disappeared from Lucy's world before.

He steadied himself against the nearest pillar and looked around for the older boy who'd been threatening him. He was nowhere to be seen.

Joe glanced down at himself to check that he wasn't still in his pyjamas. Once again, he was wearing Roman clothes. Even though it had happened before, he still found it weird. This time, he had some kind of long-sleeved shirt underneath his tunic, and he could feel an extra layer beneath the skirt of it too. He lifted the hem to have a look. There was a pair of long, close-fitting shorts over his underclothes.

At that moment, he heard a noise. He glanced

up. Lucy had just come out of the south wing.

"Pssst!" he whispered.

She turned round. "Joe? Is that you?" She looked around to see if either of them had been noticed, then hurried along the colonnade towards him. "It is! You're back!" To his astonishment, she hugged him.

"Hi, Lucy." He felt suddenly shy.

She smiled. "I'd forgotten you decided to call me that. I like it." She took his arm. "Come with me. We can't talk here, not after what happened last time. We don't want anyone to see you." She steered him back around the western end of the south wing. "I have a secret place in the gardens. We can hide there for a bit. I'll go first, you follow me, not too close."

She let go of him and set off purposefully down the lawns beyond the palace. About halfway down the slope, she cut across to the east. Joe followed at a safe distance, trying to keep bushes and tree trunks between him and the palace as much as possible, in case anyone was looking out. Finally, she disappeared into a kind of shrubbery. Joe looked around one last time and then ducked in after her.

"Hopefully, nobody will find us here," she said in a low voice. "Apart from the gardeners, the only person I know who comes here is Antonia." She settled herself on the outstretched branch of one of the shrubs. Joe looked around and spied a stump to sit on. Lucy gazed at him, shaking her head. "I can't believe you're here! You know, I was just thinking about you a few moments before you appeared."

"That's funny. I was thinking about you too, sort of." He grinned sheepishly. "Do you think that's how it happened, then?"

"How what happened?"

"How I came to be here again - by both of us thinking about each other at the same moment?"

"Maybe. I don't know." She bounced up and down gently on the branch. "I've thought about you quite a lot over the last three months."

Joe frowned. "But it's only been three weeks."

"No it hasn't. You were here in July before, and now it's October."

Joe looked around. The leaves of the shrubs were turning red and orange, and now that he thought about it, there was that sweet autumn smell in the air.

"I'd pretty much given up hoping you'd come," Lucy said.

"I don't get it." Joe scratched his head. "At home, it's only the middle of August." They looked at one another. "It's also night time," he said. "I was in bed when I suddenly appeared here." It occurred to him that he should be feeling tired, but he wasn't at all.

"So what did you do?"

"Nothing, as far as I know. I was thinking about you, and about this place. But there's nothing new about that. We even went to the museum again today, and I tried to get back here through the dolphin mosaic like last time."

"What dolphin mosaic?"

Joe laughed. "Of course! You wouldn't know about that!" It could be fun knowing a few things Lucy didn't, he thought. Otherwise, it was him asking all the questions, and her with all the answers. "I guess you won't ever see it, though," he added thoughtfully.

"What are you talking about?"

"In ninety or a hundred years, the people living here are going to put down a beautiful mosaic in the room I landed in last time. It's what this palace will be famous for when the rest of it has disappeared."

"How do you know that?" Lucy didn't seem impressed.

"Because I'm from the future, well, from here it's the future. It's 2014 back at home."

"It can't be!" She looked horrified. "Why didn't you tell me that before?"

Joe thought about it. "I don't know really. I suppose I was a bit surprised to land up here. I didn't know where I was. But now I've read lots of books about your time, and looked it up on the internet as well."

"What are books?"

"Books?" Joe smiled. "I'd forgotten you don't have them. They're lots of bits of paper held together in a bundle, with things written on each page."

"Like scrolls?"

"Yes, kind of, but flat."

"And what's the internet?"

"The internet -" He paused. This was much more difficult. "Well, the internet is like the biggest book you could ever imagine, only it doesn't actually exist anywhere, on paper or anything, and you only look at the bits you want, on a computer or a mobile or something."

Lucy's brow was furrowed with concentration. "What's a computer?"

"It's a kind of machine," Joe began again. "Oh, never mind! I can't explain and it doesn't matter anyway. None of it will be invented for nearly two thousand years." He shrugged nonchalantly, but he was suddenly proud of the progress made by his parents' and grandparents' generations, even though it had nothing to do with him.

Lucy was looking at him through narrowed eyes, however. "I was right about you when we first met. You *are* an evil spirit after all!"

"No, I'm not! Come on, Lucy! I'm just Joe."

"So you say." But she still looked at him with suspicion.

"Look, it really doesn't matter where I come from. The main thing is, I'm here! I've been wanting to come back pretty much since the moment I left."

"That's the other thing -" Lucy had stopped bouncing on the branch. "What happened to you? You never came back to meet me like we agreed."

Joe had the feeling that she'd just remembered

she was supposed to be cross with him.

"I don't know what happened," he said. "I was standing on the colonnade, where I appeared just now, and a boy with curly, black hair came and started talking to me. It was quite scary actually." He wished at once that he hadn't admitted this.

But Lucy's expression changed from annoyance to worry. "Did you say anything to him?"

Joe nodded. "I totally forgot that I wasn't supposed to talk. He wanted to know what my name was."

"What did you say?"

"I can't remember. But it wasn't what you'd said. I just blurted out the first three names I could think of. He knew straight away I was lying."

"Oh no!" She wrapped her arms tightly around herself, as though she were cold. "That was Tiberius, in case you didn't realise. He can be really nasty. We don't want him to know anything about you this time!"

"Well, I'm going to need a new story anyway, if I've been away so long," Joe said. "And it needs to be a better one than last time. It's no good if I'm not allowed to talk or I have to hide the whole time."

"I know, I know! It wasn't a very good plan before. I didn't think it would matter, but it did."

"So did they notice I'd gone?" he asked.

"My mother did. By that time, it was just as well you had. She'd said something to my aunt about adopting a mute boy, and of course my aunt didn't know what she was talking about."

"I was afraid that would happen," Joe said.

"Yes, I should have thought of it. It just seemed like a bit of fun when I said it."

"Did you get into trouble then?"

"Mmmm." Lucy looked at her feet.

"What happened?"

"I got a whipping," she said quietly.

"Oh no!" A cold shiver ran over Joe. "That's dreadful!"

Lucy shrugged. "The boys get whipped if they don't get their lessons right. I'm lucky it hasn't happened to me before."

"What did you say about who I was?"

"I told them I didn't know - which is sort of true, isn't it? I said you'd turned up at the same time as everyone else, and that you'd told me you were my cousin."

"So if I'm supposed to have lied to you," Joe said, "why did you get punished? Surely that wasn't your fault!"

"No." Lucy sighed. "Unfortunately, there was a slave boy who ran away from a villa near here at the same time. They were convinced that was you. Do you remember the ship we saw coming in that day? They thought you were going to try and stow away on it. But when they searched it, they couldn't find you or him. So they punished me instead, for playing with a slave."

Joe said nothing for a few moments. Nobody back in his own world had even known he'd gone. He might not be able to choose when he slipped through time, but the only kinds of consequences in his own life were things like Dad getting cross with him for standing on the mosaic. It hadn't occurred to him that Lucy might get into real trouble because of him.

"Are you sure you want me to stay, this time?" he asked.

"Oh yes!" Lucy looked up at him. "I was cross with you for a couple of weeks after you'd gone, especially as you didn't say goodbye. But the slave thing wasn't your fault, just unlucky. Once my skin had healed and the bruising had gone down, I started to hope you'd come back."

"Why?"

"I like you," she said. "You're different, interesting. You probably think I have everything, but actually my life is often really boring."

"Really?"

"We never go anywhere - I haven't left the palace compound since we moved here - and we don't have friends. We hardly ever have visitors, except for people coming to see my father. I know we had my cousins here, and some of them stayed for over a month, but I didn't like any of them as much as you. Once they went though, it seemed even more boring than before."

Joe felt something warm in his chest. He was

pleased that Lucy liked him so much. He thought about telling her that he liked her too, but decided it would sound soppy, even though it was true.

"What about Tiberius?" he said instead. "What did he say about me disappearing right in front of him?"

Lucy grimaced. "Nothing at all. I didn't even know you'd seen him. That's the trouble with Tiberius. He's always storing up information to use against you later on."

"So we don't know if I faded away, or vanished into thin air? Or if I seemed to go deaf and walked off? We don't know anything?"

Lucy shook her head. "The only thing we can do is arrange things this time so that he doesn't realise you're the same person."

"But he'll recognise me! You did."

She thought for a minute. "Maybe not if we dye your hair. Children never dye their hair, so he won't expect that."

"How are we going to do that then?"

"We'll ask Arethusa again. She'll know how to do it."

"Okay, then what? Why are you smiling?"

"Okay," said Lucy. "The next thing is that you have you stop saying 'okay'!"

Joe laughed. "Okay! That's my last one, I promise."

"Hmmm," said Lucy.

"Really! I'll try properly now. Actually, since I was last here, I've been noticing how often people say it at home. So at least I do hear it ... mostly."

"We'll see." She didn't sound convinced.

There was a sound nearby. Joe stood stock still.

"What was that?" he whispered.

Lucy stood up silently and tiptoed to the edge of the shrubbery. "It's alright," she said, turning back towards him. "It's only one of the slaves doing some pruning."

"Is that okay, though - I mean, is it alright? He might have heard us talking."

She shrugged. "Even if he did, it's quite likely he doesn't speak enough Latin to understand. Gardening's the kind of job they give to the uneducated slaves."

Joe dug with his toe in the soil at the foot of one of the shrubs. "Why would you educate a slave?"

"You wouldn't!" She laughed. "But as Rome conquers new lands, the army takes prisoners. And those prisoners are sent as slaves to other parts of the empire."

She held up her hand before Joe could speak. "I know you think it's wrong. But it's the way things are here. You'll have to get used to it if you're staying."

She went back to her branch. "The educated ones are used as teachers and scribes. I think we might need the help of one or two of them, as well as Arethusa."

Joe frowned. "Can you trust them?"

"I think so. They're used to keeping their master's secrets. And there are a few who definitely like me, so if we stick with them, we should be safe."

"What are we going to get them to do, then?" Joe asked.

Lucy tapped the side of her nose with her finger. "I've had an idea," she said.

7

"The important thing is to come up with a good reason for you being here in the first place. I think you need a letter of introduction." Lucy stood up and began to pace around in the small space between the shrubs.

"You need to be seen arriving as well," she went on. "We don't know how long you're going to be here, but we need to do it properly this time."

"So how are we going to manage that?"

"I think I'll ask Septimus to help us. He's one of the scribes. He could write a letter from your mother asking if you can stay here, because she's suddenly been taken ill."

"Who am I this time?" Joe asked dubiously.

Lucy thought for a moment, then clasped her hands together, clearly pleased with herself. "My mother had a friend when we lived in Verulamium. She was called Severina Orbiana," she said. "She moved away to the north, but she had a son the same age as me. If your hair was black, you might look a bit like him. In any case, we haven't seen him in seven years so it doesn't matter if you don't look exactly right. My mother wouldn't expect to recognise you."

"Who's going to deliver this letter?"

"You are. You carry it with you."

"And do I arrive here alone with it?" Joe asked.

Lucy walked a few more paces round the circle. "No, they'd expect you to travel with a slave. But you can say he took ill and died just before you got to Noviomagus. I'm not sure quite how far that is from here, only about half an hour, I think - the slaves walk there and back in a morning if they've been sent on an errand."

Joe nodded. Noviomagus must be Chichester. He wondered for a moment about the name. He'd always thought Roman town names ended in chester, like Chichester. But it seemed not. "How will I get there?" he asked.

"We'll ask Septimus if anyone is riding out early tomorrow morning. They can take you, and you can walk back."

"Wouldn't I have some kind of luggage?" Joe pointed out.

"That's true. We'll ask Arethusa to pack you a bag. If you were travelling a long way, you wouldn't want to be carrying very much, so it can be quite simple."

"What's my name, then?"

Lucy frowned. "I'm not completely certain. You're the eldest son, so the first two names would be the same as your father's, which I think are Marcus Placidius. I know your *cognomen* is Valentinian. I remember my mother had a letter from Severina Orbiana before we moved here, so I'll try and check."

"You remember a single letter?"

"Of course! They're really rare. Someone has to carry them, so they cost a lot to send. Anyway, if I'm right, I think I know where it would be, so I'll creep in and find it. I'll go and find Arethusa as well. Wait here, I won't be long."

Lucy slipped out through the bushes, leaving Joe alone. He watched through the leaves as she ran up the lawn to the palace. Then he got up and went over to her branch. He bounced a little, like she'd been doing, but then stopped, afraid that it would make the leaves of the shrub wave around. He made circles in the dirt with the toe of his sandal and wondered how to pass the time.

It occurred to him that he might usefully inspect his clothes to see exactly what he was wearing and to make sure he knew how to do all the fastenings. Nothing should be left to chance this time. So he undid and did up his sandals, then took off his belt and tunic, and checked his shirt, shorts and underwear, before putting the tunic back on.

Lucy was gone some time. Joe was just beginning to worry when he heard footsteps on the grass nearby. He sat completely still.

"It's only me!" she said, pushing the branches aside. "Sorry it took so long. Arethusa will be here in a few minutes with everything she needs for your hair. There isn't really anywhere else we can risk doing it."

She brandished a scroll of something like papyrus. "I found this though! Shall we have a lesson on your family, or at least your family as it was four years ago when she wrote? My mother may well ask after everyone."

Lucy snapped a twig from one of the shrubs, and began to scratch the ground with it, pausing to refer to the scroll now and then. Joe watched as she drew a family tree on the bare earth between them. After a minute, he said, "Why don't you give me the twig? I'll remember better if I write their names myself, and you'll have both hands to hold that open to read. I'm not very good at Roman numerals either, so it would be easier for me if I wrote down their ages my way."

Lucy handed the twig to him, and sat down on the stump, puzzling over the numbers Joe wrote beside each name.

"Let me make sure I've got this right," he said, when they'd finished. "After me, there's Placidia, who was born the year before they left Verulamium. She's now eight. Then there is Claudia who is now six, and Gregorius who had just been born when this letter was written. So he must be four. Shall we add an extra child?"

"If you like."

"Let's have a two year old boy, then. Give me a name."

"Quintilius," Lucy said, "since he's the fifth child."

"Right." Joe scratched the name in the ground. "Have I spelled that right?"

"That's fine. You can put one 'l' or two, it doesn't matter."

"And what's the name of the place where they are now?"

"Mancunium."

Joe grinned. "Manchester!"

Lucy looked blank. "If you say so. Marcus Placidius is a General in the army. That's where he was posted, and they were still there four years ago. We don't know for sure that they haven't moved since. But my mother wouldn't know that either."

"So my father wouldn't be married to my mother then?" Joe said. "I read that in a few of the books, about soldiers not being allowed to marry until they retire."

"That's true," Lucy said. "But lots of soldiers have families living outside the forts. That's how it was in Verulamium. You would still see him fairly often - probably as often as I see my father - and you'd still call him 'Pater'."

There was a quiet cough on the edge of the shrubbery.

"That'll be Arethusa." Lucy put her head through between the branches. "In here," she whispered.

Arethusa appeared with a bucket of water and a basket. "Master Joe!" she exclaimed in astonishment. "What are you doing here?"

"Hello, Arethusa!" Joe beamed. "I'm back!" Knowing people here made him feel at home somehow.

"But we need to do things differently this time," Lucy said sternly.

"Of course, Miss Lucilia." Arethusa bowed her head at once.

"This time, he's Valentinian, the son of my mother's old friend. He's going to need practice answering to his new name, so it would help if you start calling him by it."

"Very well, Miss. So I'm to dye Master Valentinian's hair?"

"That's right," Lucy said. "He needs to look different."

Arethusa nodded.

"What do you want me to do?" Joe asked.

"You're fine sitting on that branch, Master Valentinian, but I need you to take off your tunic and shirt. We don't want to get dye on them." Arethusa took a drape from the basket. "We need to cover your skin too, as much as we can. Wrap this round you. I've got some cloths for your face and neck as well. Once it's taken, the dye doesn't come off."

She took a long strip of material from the basket and wrapped it around his hairline from the back of his neck, up behind his ears to meet in the middle of his forehead. "Could you hold that a moment for me, Miss Lucilia?" Arethusa delved in her basket and brought out a metal clip which she used to hold the cloth in place.

"Ouch," Joe grumbled. "That hurts."

She adjusted it and pushed another piece of cloth behind. "Is that better?"

"A bit."

"Stop fussing, Joe!" Lucy said.

"It's Valentinian, remember," he said irritably. "Anyway, it's alright for you! I must look ridiculous, with my ears sticking out like this!"

"Well we don't want them getting black."

Joe watched Arethusa take out a paintbrush from the basket and uncork the bottle of dye. The air was immediately filled with the most revolting stench.

"My God!" he exclaimed. "What is in that? It smells like something's died!"

"It has!" Lucy was holding her nose, but she was laughing too. "Don't breathe in!"

"You could have warned me! What is it then?"

"Tell him, Arethusa!"

Arethusa's eyes danced. "It's dead leeches. They've been rotted in red wine for forty days."

Joe clamped his hand to his mouth and nose. "That's disgusting! I think I'm going to be sick!"

"Don't be daft!" Lucy said. "Just don't breathe through your nose again."

"What? Ever?"

"No, stupid! The smell should escape upwards from the bushes. This is why we have to do it here."

Arethusa dipped the brush into the bottle and began to paint Joe's hair. He felt the thick, cold drops of dye trickle on to his scalp.

"How long do I have to keep it on?" he asked, when she'd finished.

"An hour, Master Valentinian."

"You're joking!"

"Of course, she isn't," Lucy said. "It has to have time to take before you wash it away. Arethusa will come back when it's time. I'm going to see Septimus about the letter. Don't go anywhere now, will you!" She giggled.

"Ha, ha," said Joe sourly.

Left alone again, he sat and fumed. He'd looked forward so much to being here again, and to seeing Lucy. But he felt like he was being punished for last time, especially since she wasn't even prepared to sit through this with him. He pinched his nostrils shut with finger and thumb and tried not to think about the scraps of rotten leech on his scalp.

The hour seemed like an eternity. He practised scratching Roman numerals in the earth, and when he'd tired of that, he wrote his new name over and over. He'd given up on that too when Arethusa eventually returned, carrying another bucket of water and a bag.

"Here's your luggage, Master Valentinian." She hung it in one of the bushes. "Ready to wash the dye out?"

"You bet!" he said. "Shouldn't we wait for Lucy, though?"

"No. This will take a while anyway. We need to rinse it several times before we soap the last of it away."

"Do I dare ask what's in the soap?"

Arethusa smiled. "Only ashes and tallow."

"Tallow is animal fat, isn't it?"

"That's right."

Joe sighed, and knelt down for her to begin rinsing. He had no idea what was in hair dye and soap at home. But he was suddenly grateful for laboratory-tested chemicals which weren't obviously bits of dead animal and other nasty stuff.

He was drying his hair on a cloth when Lucy appeared again.

"It's all done!" She waved another scroll triumphantly. "Septimus even managed to peel the seal off the other letter and stick it on here."

"Good."

"You don't sound very pleased."

"I've just spent an hour sitting in a poisonous cloud *on my own*." He gave extra emphasis to the last three words to make sure she understood. But she just grinned.

"It's good though," she said. "You do look completely different. You've done a great job, Arethusa!"

"Thank you, Miss Lucilia." Arethusa picked up the empty buckets and the basket of stained cloths. "I should go. I need to get rid of all this."

"Of course. Please just remember when you meet him again that you've never seen Valentinian before."

"Yes, Miss." Arethusa bowed, then pushed her way out through the bushes.

"So what happens now?" Joe asked.

"Well, it depends a bit on how you smell!" Lucy laughed. "Septimus said it would be safer for you to go down to the shore and walk along the coast to the footpath. He said it takes you up to the main road, so you can come along from there. He thought we shouldn't risk you being seen riding out from here to Noviomagus."

"That's all fine, but what does it have to do with how I smell?" Even though he knew Lucy was talking about the dye, Joe still felt slightly offended.

Lucy laughed again. "You can't be seen wandering around the palace between now and when you arrive formally. But you can't present yourself to my mother still smelling of hair dye."

"I could have a swim in the sea," Joe suggested.

"No, that's no good. Then you'd smell of salt

water, and there's no sea between here and Noviomagus, so that wouldn't make sense on your journey."

"What shall I do, then?" Joe felt himself getting tetchy. Why was nothing ever simple with Lucy?

"Let's go down to the shore first, and see how you are once we're away from these bushes. There's so much dye still soaking away, it's hard to tell how much of the smell is from you."

"Great," Joe said sarcastically. "In that case, I'm going first this time. You follow me." He stomped off huffily down the lawn. When he reached the shore, he picked up a stone and skimmed it across the water.

A minute or two later, Lucy joined him. "You forgot your luggage!" She put the bag down beside him. "You don't smell too bad at all, actually."

"Thanks!"

"No, I mean it."

"Yeah, right. I smell of grease and wine. Delicious!"

"That's alright though," she said. "We use both for cleaning, so to me, you just smell clean."

"Really?" He was incredulous. "This place is mad!"

Lucy shook her head at him.

"Right, then." Joe skimmed one last stone across the sea. "What do I do?"

"You take your bag and this letter - you might want to bash it up a little bit so it looks like you've been carrying it with you for a long time - and you walk along the shoreline about quarter of an hour that way, until you come to a path that leads inland."

"How long would I have been travelling in total?" Joe asked.

"I don't know. Maybe two weeks? It's a long way to walk."

"No kidding! And what do I do when I get here?"

"Just come straight down the road, and you'll arrive at the main entrance. Ask the slave for an audience with Helena Calvina - that's my mother. Present your letter to her, and then try to act naturally!"

Joe swallowed.

"Go on then. The sooner you do it, the sooner it's over!" Lucy handed him the bag and the scroll, then squeezed his arm. "You'll be fine! See you soon! Good luck!"

Joe took a deep breath and started off along the shore away from her.

8

The path from the sea up to the road was fortunately quite obvious. There were sand dunes to either side, and Joe paused to roll the scroll and his leather bag in the dust at the edge of the path to make them look more worn. The edges of the scroll weren't crumbly like he'd expected. Perhaps that was because it was fresh rather than centuries old as these things were in museums.

The road was wide and paved with flat stones, and it was completely straight. He could see the palace down at the end of it, although it was still quite a long way away. As he came close to it, he felt his heart pounding. Nothing he'd ever done before had prepared him for this. When he'd taken tests at school, or piano exams, he'd known exactly what was expected of him. This was more like acting in a play when you didn't know your own lines or what anyone else would say, or even what was going to happen next.

The entrance to the palace was in the centre of

the building, exactly as the guide at Fishbourne had described. Behind the pillars, enormous oak doors barred the way. But in one of them was cut an ordinary-sized door. Joe hammered on it loudly. He trembled while he waited for it to be answered.

A guard in a helmet and a leather breast-plate opened the door. He held a kind of spear in one hand. "Ave!" he barked. "What is your business here?"

"Ave." Joe wondered if he should drop down on one knee, but decided against it. "I am come to seek an audience with Helena Calvina. I bring this letter for her." He blinked, startled at the words which had come out of his own mouth. Hopefully, they sounded convincing in Latin.

"Wait here." The guard took the letter and closed the door. Joe waited, trying to stay calm.

After a few minutes, the door opened again.

"Follow me!" The guard led the way smartly through two arches, and around a small ornamental pool set in the floor. Joe glanced around as he hurried after the man. Marble columns supported the roof of the hall, and the walls were painted from floor to ceiling with pictures of birds and fruit.

"Wow!" he murmured to himself. If only Dad could see this.

On the other side of the entrance hall, they emerged into the colonnade along the east wing. Ahead of them, the path continued straight up the middle of the formal gardens to the west wing. But the guard turned left, and continued around to the south side, and along to the hall where the supper party had been last time Joe was here.

"Her Ladyship will receive you in her suite," the guard said. He opened a door at the end of the hall, and then another door beyond it. Stepping into the room, he bowed low. "The young man who brought the letter, may it please your Ladyship."

"Very good. Send him in."

Joe stepped forward.

Lucy's mother lounged on a long couch in the most beautiful room Joe had yet seen. It was light and open, looking out into a courtyard bursting with palms. Beyond, you could see the informal gardens sloping away, and then the sea. A slave massaged her feet while she sipped her drink from a tall, silver goblet.

Joe bowed low. He wished he'd had the chance to look in a mirror, to reassure himself that he really did look different. It was hard to believe that Helena Calvina wouldn't recognise him. He wondered if she noticed his legs shaking beneath his tunic.

"Welcome, Valentinian," she said. "I am happy to receive news of your mother, though sad that illness is the cause of your visit. She won't be coming to the feast, I presume."

What feast? Joe looked at her, hoping his panic didn't show in his face. Lucy hadn't mentioned anything. "No, your Ladyship," he said, as calmly as he could. "She remembers you fondly, however," he added, bowing his head.

"And I her." Lucy's mother pulled some grapes from a bunch beside her. "She has five children now, I see."

"That is correct, your Ladyship." Joe wondered whether to say something further about the family, but decided not to risk it.

"What ails her, may I ask?"

Joe caught his breath again. He and Lucy hadn't discussed what might be the matter with Severina Orbiana. Presumably, Septimus hadn't included anything specific in the letter either, or Helena Calvina wouldn't have asked.

"She has been weak ever since the birth of -" He tried to remember the name of the extra child he and Lucy had invented. "- my youngest brother," he finished, hoping Helena Calvina wouldn't notice his hesitation.

He tried to think what illnesses the Romans had had. There hadn't been much about it in his books. "She suffers from sweats and sickness," he said, parroting the kind of language he'd heard in period dramas on the television. "I'm sorry to say she can no longer rise from her bed."

It sounded surprisingly believable. He felt pleased with himself. Perhaps he should become an actor, one day.

Lucy's mother seemed satisfied. "You may of course stay as long as you need. Did you travel alone?"

"My slave fell ill two days ago, before we reached Noviomagus. He is dead." It felt strange to state this fact so baldly. But Joe was afraid that pretending to be upset might be a mistake.

"That is a pity," Lucy's mother said, in a voice entirely without pity. "Never mind. My children's nursemaid can look after you."

She rang a tiny gold bell. "Bring me Arethusa," she said to the slave who appeared at her side. And then to Joe, "I don't know whether you remember my daughter, Sallustia Lucilia. She is the same age as you. You were both infants when you last met. She will be your guide."

"Thank you, your Ladyship." Joe bowed his head again. "That is extremely kind."

He was bursting with excitement as he and Arethusa left Helena Calvina's rooms.

"It worked!" he whispered. "Oh, Arethusa, it worked! That's amazing! Thank you! Thank you for helping me!"

Arethusa's face remained impassive. "Very good, Master Valentinian," she said.

"Oh, come on! At least smile!"

Arethusa stopped walking and looked at him. "We all have our part to play, Master Valentinian," she said quietly. "I play mine. You must play yours." Without waiting for him to answer, she walked on again.

Joe followed, trying to decide whether she had been telling him off or warning him.

She went through a doorway into a small room. "Excuse me, Miss Lucilia." She curtsied. "May I present Marcus Placidius Valentinian, eldest son of her Ladyship's friend, Severina Orbiana."

Lucy stepped forward and gave Joe her hand. "Pleased to meet you," she said, with a curtsey.

"What are you doing?" Joe said. "There's nobody here but us."

"It's practice," she hissed. "Bow your head and say, 'The pleasure is mine'."

Joe giggled. "The pleasure is mine." He dropped her hand. "There. Happy now?"

"I hope you do better when we introduce you to the rest of the family," Lucy said, speaking normally again. "Where will he sleep, Arethusa?"

"Her Ladyship told me to put him in the room at the end of the passage. I'm going to prepare it now."

"Well, that'll be better than the linen closet!" Lucy grinned. "Come on, then. Let's go and have a tour of the palace, just like we would if you'd never been here before. Arethusa will take your bag for you."

Obediently, Joe trotted after Lucy as she set off around the compound, gesturing to right and left, telling him what each building was. After about ten minutes, however, he was beginning to get bored. "Give up, Lucy!" he whispered. "I know most of this already."

"I know you do! It's for show."

"Who's watching?"

"You never know." A couple of minutes later, however, she relented. "Let's go round to the garden."

"That reminds me of something," Joe said. "I was going to ask you if there's a stream and a pond somewhere?"

"Yes, there is. Why do you want to know?"

"Someone I met told me there might be. I just wanted to see if they were right."

Lucy frowned. "Who have you been talking to?"

"Nobody you would know."

Together, they went back around the end of the south wing to the garden. A robin sang in one of the trees.

"You know, I feel much better," Joe said. "I feel much more - I don't know - real. It's like I was just sketched into the picture before, and now I'm in full colour."

Lucy laughed. "You do say some funny things."

"I can't really explain it properly," he said. "But it's so nice not to have to hide, to be allowed to be here talking to you. I don't feel as though I might vanish at any moment."

"I don't understand you." Lucy pulled a leaf from a tree as they passed. "Last time, you were worried about not being able to get back to wherever it is you're from."

"I know. But this time, I know that'll be alright,

so I want to stay as long as I can." He thought for a moment. "What shall we do about explaining that I've gone, when I do disappear?"

For the first time since they'd talked about Tiberius, Lucy looked worried. "I don't know. I'll think of something when it happens. Let's not bother about it now."

"But last time, you were punished," Joe persisted.

"That's not your problem," she snapped. "Forget about it. We can't plan for it because we don't know when it will be. I'll come up with something."

Joe fell silent.

They came to the pond the guide had mentioned. A stream trickled down from it towards the sea.

"If the water is always running out of this pond," Joe said, "how does it stay full?"

"I don't know. I suppose there must be an underground spring." Lucy wasn't cross any more, he saw. He was glad. Other girls he knew sulked for ages when they were upset.

She took her sandals off. "Let's make a dam."

Joe sat down on the bank and took his sandals off as well. Together they began to build walls across the sandy bed of the stream, diverting the course of the water around obstacles and through channels.

After a while, Joe looked up. "There are some children coming," he whispered.

Lucy stopped what she was doing and

straightened up. "Don't worry. You survived my mother on your own, this is easy. Hello, you two!" she called out. "Do you remember Valentinian, Petrus? The son of mother's friend in Verulamium? Valentinian, this is my brother Petrus, and my sister Antonia."

"Hello." Petrus and Antonia smiled and nodded.

"Valentinian's staying with us for a while. His mother's ill." Petrus and Antonia nodded again.

"What are you doing there? Is there some plan to it?" Petrus asked, pointing to the embankments of sand and pebbles.

"Not specially. Joe and I -" Lucy coughed to cover her mistake. "We thought we might dig a deep pool over here. Valentinian wanted to make a whirlpool, didn't you?"

"That's right." Joe wondered if Petrus was looking at him especially closely, but decided that he was being paranoid.

"Can we help?" Antonia asked.

"If you like." Joe smiled at her.

The four of them worked companionably together for some time.

"Do you have brothers and sisters, Valentinian?" Antonia asked after a while.

"Two sisters and two brothers," Joe said. He was about to reel off their names and ages when he realised that it might sound rather unnatural. "I'm the eldest."

"Lucky you!" Antonia pulled a face. "I hate

being the youngest."

Just in time, Joe stopped himself from agreeing with her. He often wished he and Sam could switch places.

"I don't know what you're grumbling about," Petrus said. "Lucilia and I don't have a particular place in the family. We're just in the middle somewhere behind Sallustia." He stood up. "Speaking of whom ..."

An older girl was walking down the lawn towards them. "It's time for supper," she called. "I told Capriola I'd fetch you all." She looked at Joe. "Hello. Who are you?"

Joe glanced at Lucy, who gave the slightest nod of her head. "I'm Valentinian," he said. "Marcus Placidius Valentinian, eldest son of Severina Orbiana."

Sallustia curtsied and held out her hand. "Pleased to meet you."

Joe took her hand and bowed. "The pleasure is mine," he said. It seemed a bit daft to be so formal when he was standing barefoot in the stream, but Sallustia didn't appear to mind.

"Supper is served," she said, and went back towards the palace.

Joe dropped behind as they walked back up the lawns, pretending to adjust the strap of his sandal. "Was that okay?" he whispered to Lucy, who had waited for him.

"Fine. Really, you're doing well," she said, "apart from asking if it was 'okay'!" She grinned.

They went past the back of the south wing to the top corner of the garden, behind the orchard.

"Where are we going?" Joe asked.

"To the outdoor triclinium," Lucy said. "It's where we eat when it's warm outside. This might be the last time this year, if the weather changes."

They came to a stone construction, three very thick walls arranged like three sides of a square, sloping outwards. The fourth side was missing and around the inside of the three walls was a high step, like a stone bench.

Seeing Joe's confusion, Lucy whispered, "It's for reclining at formal meals. But this is just a family supper, so most of us will sit on the step."

Joe nodded and sat down beside Lucy. Petrus, Antonia and Sallustia had taken their places already. There was the sound of voices approaching. Helena Calvina walked arm in arm with a man that Joe supposed must be Lucy's father. Behind them came two older boys.

Joe recognised Tiberius at once. He felt his knees tremble as they had done standing in front of Lucy's mother earlier in the afternoon. He stood up.

"Ah, here he is," Helena Calvina said. "Marcus Placidius Valentinian. Valentinian, this is my husband, governor of Britannia, Gaius Sallustius Lucullus."

Joe bowed his head and dropped to one knee.

"Very good!" said Lucy's father, smiling. "Stand up!"

Joe stood.

"These are my sons, Marius and Tiberius."

Joe bowed. "Pleased to meet you." He looked up as briefly as he could without seeming rude, determined not to catch Tiberius' eye.

"The pleasure is mine," they both replied.

"Excellent! Let's eat!" Lucullus and Helena Calvina reclined side by side on cushions already set out for them, supporting themselves on one elbow. Tiberius and Marius sat on the step to the right. Feet and hands were washed, and then the slaves sprang forward with platters, offering food first to Lucullus and Helena Calvina, before turning to each member of the family from oldest to youngest.

Joe kept his eyes on his lap and took his cue from Lucy. He felt sure that Tiberius was watching him, but he didn't say anything.

The supper seemed to go on and on. By the time it was over, the air had grown cool and dark, and the way back to the terraces of the south wing was marked by burning torches. Joe could hear the murmuring of the sea as he walked beside Lucy across grass which was now wet with dew.

"I think that went alright, didn't it?" he said.

Lucy nodded. "You'll get used to it."

From the shadows beyond the flaming torches, a voice said, "That's if you stay around long enough this time."

Joe and Lucy swung round in the direction of

the voice. In the gloom, Joe could just make out the curly hair and cruel smile of Tiberius. The older boy lounged against a wall with his arms folded. His eyes glinted in the torchlight.

"What do you mean?" Joe said. His own voice sounded squeaky.

"I think you know perfectly well. All this about you being Marcus Placidius' son? It's a lie. Last time, it was Iovinus, wasn't it? And really, it's Joe. I've heard you talking to each other. You call her Lucy, don't you? It's rather sweet, in its way. But who are you actually? Or rather, *what* are you?"

"You're talking nonsense," Lucy said. She stuck her chin out. "You didn't live with us when we were in Verulamium. You wouldn't remember Severina Orbiana's son." Her voice quivered.

"Perhaps your friend would like to answer the question himself," Tiberius said. "Last time I asked him, I suddenly found I was talking to the air."

Joe looked levelly at Tiberius. "I am Marcus Placidius Valentinian," he said with all the determination he could muster. "And I have been welcomed into this house by Helena Calvina herself." He tugged Lucy's arm. "Goodnight, Tiberius. May the evil spirits remain at bay." He looked Tiberius in the eye. To his surprise, the older boy looked away at once.

"Don't threaten me!" he snarled. Then he turned on his heel and stalked off into the darkness.

9

When Joe awoke the next morning, he lay for nearly a minute with his eyes closed. If he was now back in his own time, he wanted to put it off a little longer, like he did when he woke from a dream he'd been enjoying.

With his other senses though, he strained to know if he was still in Lucy's world. There was no sound in the room, which might just mean that Sam had got up to go to the loo, though he couldn't hear any traffic outside either. And his back ached just as it had after the night he'd spent in Arethusa's linen closet. He felt around with his hands. This definitely wasn't Dad's sofa-bed.

He opened his eyes. He was still in the room he'd been given in the south wing of the palace. He threw back the covers and jumped out of bed, leaping around the small room and hooting in a lap of victory.

There was a tap at the door. Joe sat down quickly. "Come in."

Arethusa entered. "Good morning, Master Valentinian. I've brought you some water to wash with."

"Thank you, Arethusa!" He beamed at her. "I'm not late getting up, am I?"

"No, I was only coming to wake you now." She set the bowl and jug down on a narrow cupboard opposite the bed. The only other furniture in the room was a chair that Joe had draped his clothes on last night. There were no pictures or ornaments anywhere. It was more like a monk's cell than any bedroom Joe had ever been into.

"I think autumn suits me better than summer." He grinned. "You woke me up painfully early last time I was here."

Arethusa pressed her lips together but said nothing.

"I know," Joe said. "I'm not supposed to mention it. But sometimes I'm bursting to say something!"

She shook her head at him. "If anyone hears you talking like that to me ..." she whispered. Her eyes were wide. With a jolt, he realised that she was frightened.

"Breakfast will be in the dining room when you're ready, Master Valentinian," she said in a normal voice. "Miss Lucilia will come and show you the way in a few minutes."

Joe poured water from the jug into the bowl. It was very cold. He washed quickly. One day, he thought, he would go and use the baths. That had looked like fun in the books he'd read. But since he couldn't go with Lucy, he didn't want to risk it just yet. If Tiberius was there, he didn't want to face him alone.

A shiver ran up the back of Joe's neck just at the thought of Tiberius. Arethusa's dye and Lucy's letter had been enough to convince Helena Calvina. But Tiberius had seen through his false identity straight away. Joe cursed himself for disappearing in front of Tiberius. At the time, he'd been grateful to escape, but there was no doubt that he'd made trouble for himself.

On the other hand, he had the impression that Tiberius had been worried by something last night. It puzzled him. Why would you tell someone not to threaten you, unless you felt they were doing exactly that?

He got dressed and sat down on the bed to wait for Lucy. It seemed to be something in those last few moments. He went over them again, trying to remember as precisely as he could: he had repeated his new name, and said something about the evil spirits staying away. And he had made himself look Tiberius in the eye when he spoke. That was all. There was nothing else.

Suddenly, it came to him what the answer might be. Perhaps Tiberius had thought that he was an evil spirit, capable of calling up others! It was reasonable enough, since Joe had vanished before his eyes. Maybe Tiberius had thought his remark about the spirits was a warning, rather than him just trying to be polite.

Joe gave a whoop and clapped his hands. What a brilliant misunderstanding! With luck, he might be able to use that as a shield against Tiberius. In any case, as long as he was still here, it was hard to see how Tiberius could do anything to expose him. After all, he could hardly send someone all the way to Manchester to ask Severina Orbiana about her son. That would take weeks.

No, the problem would come afterwards, when Joe had slipped back into his own time again. Then people might start listening to Tiberius' suspicions. The thought of where that would leave Lucy made Joe shudder.

At that moment, she came into the room. "Oh good, you're ready. Shall we go?"

"Hang on a minute," Joe said. "I wanted to talk to you first, while there's nobody else around. I've been thinking about Tiberius last night."

"Me too." Lucy looked unhappy.

"No, it's okay. I mean -" He grimaced. Remembering not to say 'okay' was harder than he'd thought. "It's alright. At least, I think so." He explained his theory.

Relief dawned on Lucy's face. "I think you might be right," she said. "And certainly he can't do anything about it. Nobody would believe him."

"The problem will be when I leave," Joe said. "I

don't know what caused me to disappear last time, unless it was that I was in danger."

"In danger of what?"

"I don't know. Tiberius hitting me maybe, or worse."

"But he was pretty nasty last night, and you're still here this morning."

"I did feel a bit fuzzy," Joe admitted. "But you were there with me, and I knew I wanted to hold on. Today, I feel stronger somehow."

"Good," Lucy said. She sounded slightly impatient. "Come on, let's go and have breakfast. They'll be expecting you for lessons with Petrus this morning, and you need to have eaten something first."

She led the way to the dining room. Again, there were couches arranged to form three sides of a square but the food was already set out on a large table on one side of the room. Neither of Lucy's parents were there, and Joe followed Lucy's example, serving himself and then sitting with his plate on his lap on the couch with Lucy and Antonia. Marius, Sallustia and Petrus sat together opposite them, while Tiberius sat alone on the third couch, scowling.

"Where do I go next?" Joe asked Lucy, when they'd finished.

"I'm going to take you to Petrus' room," she said. "I don't know what his lessons are for today, so it's best if you go with him."

"What might it be?"

"There's reading and writing, arithmetic and Greek."

Joe pulled a face.

"What's the matter?"

"I don't know any Greek."

"Really?" Lucy looked surprised.

"Nobody learns Greek at home, or at least, nobody I know."

"Oh well. There's all the physical training as well."

"Like what?"

"I don't really know. I've seen Petrus throwing spears and riding. Since there are two of you nearly the same size, you might do some sword practice or something like that. I've seen Tiberius and Marius sword fighting and boxing together. Here we are." She stopped at her brother's room. "Petrus, can you look after -" Joe heard her catch herself just in time to avoid saying his name. "- Valentinian today?"

Petrus nodded. "Let's go, shall we? It's the boring stuff first, then riding later."

Joe gulped. "I've never ridden a horse, not properly."

Petrus grinned. "Everyone has to start some time. It's not till after the midday meal anyway."

They walked along the colonnades and through one of the east wing courtyards to a room behind. It was small, plain and rather dark. From a cupboard in the corner, Petrus fetched two wooden boxes, each tied with a leather thong on one side. "Wax tablet and stylus," he said, handing a box to Joe with a thing like a metal pen. Joe took them casually, as though he'd used them every day for years. Petrus gestured to a bench for Joe to sit down.

"It makes a change to have company," he said, sitting down next to him. "Since my cousins left, it's been just me on my own again."

"What about your brothers?"

"They're so far ahead of me, we can't have lessons together."

Joe swallowed, relieved that Tiberius wouldn't be having classes with them.

"They're doing oratory rather than dictation," Petrus was saying. "I've got another three years before I start that. So they do physical training with Heraclio while I do dictation, arithmetic and Greek with Epistolio. And then we swap round."

He opened his wooden box to reveal two rectangular frames filled with yellowish-brown wax. Joe opened his own box. The wax was hard and smooth. He fiddled with his stylus. "Ouch!"

Petrus laughed. "Mind the point! It's sharp!"

Joe blushed. He was going to give himself away if he wasn't careful.

"You haven't had much schooling, then?" Petrus asked.

Joe hesitated. "Not a lot." Six years in his own time should count for something, he thought, but it was obvious already that he wouldn't be able to do a lot of the things Petrus had learnt. He couldn't even be sure about the stuff that ought to be okay: he had no idea how his spelling of Latin would turn out, since he didn't even know he was speaking it; and as for arithmetic, he could add up and subtract perfectly well, but his grip on Roman numerals was shaky, and he didn't know how you would do large sums with an abacus. He hadn't used one of those since he was about three years old.

"I don't know whether Lucilia said anything about Epistolio to you," Petrus said. "But you don't mess around with him. He may be a slave, but -" He jumped to his feet abruptly. "Good morning, Sir."

A man with greying hair and bushy eyebrows had entered the room.

Joe stood up too, but said nothing, unsure whether to introduce himself, and if so, how.

"Good morning, Petrus. Good morning, Valentinian. Her Ladyship has informed me that you will join my pupil's lessons for as long as you are here."

"Thank you, Sir." Joe bowed his head. Both boys sat down again.

Epistolio remained standing and cleared his throat. "Shall we begin?" His eyes were pale blue and his gaze direct. Joe felt like a mouse that has been spotted by a kestrel.

"Please take down the following dictation from

Pliny's *Naturalis Historia*, Volume 3, Book 8." To Joe's surprise, he launched into a passage about keeping fish, reciting the words slowly as he walked back and forth in front of them, without referring to any book.

Joe tried to keep up, glad that he at least understood the gist of it. But writing with the stylus was much more difficult than he'd expected. The wax was so solid that he had to press down really hard with the point of the stylus, and the letters came out awkward and jerky.

After a few words, he could feel the muscles in his hand starting to ache. After two sentences, he put the stylus down and wiggled his fingers. He glanced over at Petrus' tablet. Lucy's brother was less than halfway down the first side of the wax. Joe, on the other hand, had almost reached the bottom of his.

He picked up his stylus again and continued in smaller letters. But he was now behind. He tried desperately to remember each phrase while he wrote the previous one. But he was writing so slowly that there was more and more to remember.

He began to panic. There was hardly any space left on the second side of his tablet, and the result looked nothing at all like what Petrus had done. Joe wrote until he could fit no more in, and then sat and watched Petrus take down the rest of the dictation. It seemed to go on and on.

Eventually, Epistolio stopped speaking and

walked around the bench behind them. Joe was aware of Petrus holding his breath.

The teacher clicked his tongue. "Mistakes, here - here - and here." He pointed to the errors in Petrus' writing. Immediately, Petrus took the other end of the stylus, which was flattened like a tiny paddle, and began to rub them out.

Epistolio looked over Joe's shoulder. Joe waited.

The teacher leaned forward. "What is this?" He walked round to stand in front of Joe, picked up the tablet and held it close to his face. "What on earth does this mean?"

Joe's heart hammered. Perhaps he had written English rather than Latin. "It's the first part of what you recited, Sir," he said, meekly. "I didn't get it all."

Epistolio glared at him over the tablet. "It is no such thing! Are you mocking me, boy?"

"No, Sir."

The teacher threw the tablet into Joe's lap. "Read it back to me, then."

Slowly, Joe began to read out the words he'd scratched in the wax. After six and a half sentences, he stopped. "That was all I managed, sir," he said in a whisper.

Epistolio narrowed his eyes. "Either your memory is very good, or this is a most elaborate joke."

"I'm sorry, Sir," Joe mumbled. He wished the ground would open up. "It isn't a joke, really. I did my best."

"If that was your best -" Epistolio's eyebrow shot up. "Nevertheless, since it's your first time, and you seem to be entirely uneducated, you shall erase everything you have written on your tablet, and copy Petrus' dictation word for word. In the meantime, Petrus and I will begin on today's Greek lesson."

Silently, Petrus passed his tablet to Joe. Joe looked at it carefully. The words were tiny by comparison to his own writing. But the biggest difference was that Petrus had written the whole dictation in capital letters.

Joe groaned inwardly. How idiotic he'd been! He'd written it the way he would at home, using small letters. But he'd never seen a Latin inscription in anything but capitals. They probably didn't use small letters at all.

He began to try and scrape the wax flat with the paddle end of the stylus. In places, he'd pressed so hard that his letters had gone right through to the wooden frame underneath. He dug in with the paddle and dragged the wax across the board, trying to fill the scratches. But now there were gaping trenches in the surface as well as the grooves of the letters.

The more he tried, the worse it got. He couldn't imagine getting it as smooth as it had been when he started. He glanced up at Epistolio. But the teacher's attention remained firmly fixed on the scroll Petrus was reading from.

Joe suppressed a sigh. If he was going to have to

do this every day, living in Lucy's time might be rather hard work. He eyed the cane propped up against the wall and remembered what she'd said about her brothers getting beaten for not knowing their lessons.

There was nothing else for it. Back and forth, he scraped, back and forth. Gradually, the wax began to soften.

10

By the end of the day, Joe was sore and weary. He had managed to copy Petrus' dictation well enough, but it had taken him so long that Epistolio was convinced that he knew nothing, and decided he would start teaching Joe from scratch. Joe knew it would be better like that, but his teacher's eagle eyes didn't miss a thing. He would have to work very hard if he was going to avoid the cane that stood ready in the corner.

The other teacher, Heraclio, was exactly the opposite. For Joe's first ever riding lesson, he lifted him up on to the back of the horse, handed him the reins, and gave the animal a slap on its backside so that it trotted off across the paddock.

There was no saddle and no stirrups, so Joe clung on with his legs. Unfortunately, the horse seemed to think this was a command and scampered around the field faster and faster until Joe fell off. Heraclio scooped him up off the ground, put him back on, and slapped the horse again. Away they went a second time. Again, Joe fell off.

After the fourth time, he was bruised and resentful.

"Don't worry!" called Heraclio happily. "You'll soon learn. Why don't you sit on the fence and watch Petrus?"

The following day, however, they began with swimming in the sea. This at least was something Joe could do, better than Petrus as it turned out.

"Not completely useless, then!" Heraclio declared.

"Is that supposed to be praise?" Joe muttered under his breath.

Lucy's brother grinned. "Make the most of it!"

In the afternoon, it was back to the classroom. This time, Epistolio set Petrus some sums to do while he watched Joe write on his tablet. Joe bent over the rows of letters, scratching each one again and again in the wax. Epistolio corrected him now and then, but seemed satisfied with Joe's work. Every time he suspected Joe's attention was wandering though, he rapped him over the knuckles with a ruler. By the time they finished in middle of the afternoon, Joe's hand was red.

On the third day, the physical training was swordsmanship. Joe was half afraid Heraclio would expect him and Petrus to begin fighting with real swords straight away. But fortunately Petrus hadn't done it before either, so the slave gave them both blunt sticks and began with footwork.

"I feel like I've hardly seen you," Lucy said that afternoon, while they were playing Noughts and Crosses in one of the courtyards.

"I know." Joe stifled a yawn. "I never imagined this when I thought about being here. I suppose if you stay somewhere longer, you get something a bit more like real life." He chalked his final cross. "I win."

"Not again!" Lucy cried in frustration. "You've won every single game! How do you do that?"

Joe tapped his nose and grinned. "Two thousand years extra practice!"

"Rubbish!" Lucy brought out a small bag. "Let's play Knucklebones."

"That doesn't sound very nice."

She rolled her eyes at him. "It's called that because you play it with sheep's knuckle bones." She emptied some small white bones on to the ground. "There are lots of different ways of playing this." She began to show him.

"I know that game," Joe said. "We call it Jacks, or Five Stones." He threw the knuckle bones up in the air and caught two of them on the back of his hand. "Ouch! It hurts less with my plastic set."

"Don't be soft!"

"I'm not!" he protested. "But you know, *everything* about the way you live is less comfortable than in my world!"

"Maybe you need to toughen up!" she retorted.

Joe harrumphed. "Maybe you need to improve some of your inventions! I mean this wax tablet and stylus thing, it's such hard work!"

Lucy narrowed her eyes. "You could always go out into the countryside and stay in one of the roundhouses," she said. "One room for everyone, a dirt floor, no windows and no way of getting clean. You'd know what hard work is then! You fetch your own water, chop your own wood, light your own fire, kill and cook your own food, and bury your own rubbish."

"Alright, alright!" Joe held up his hand. "I get the point."

"Do you?" She fixed him with a look. "I think you'd find this pretty comfortable after that."

"Yes, alright! You're probably right." He folded his arms. "Anyway, how do you know what it's like out there? You've never lived like that."

"We stopped off when we travelled down from Verulamium. My father wanted us to see what Rome has given the people of Britannia."

"But if they're still living in roundhouses, it hasn't given them anything!" Joe said.

"Only in the countryside. In the towns it's more like here, proper houses, running water, baths, all that sort of thing."

She sounded so smug, Joe thought, as though it had anything to do with her. He yawned.

"You're not tired, are you?" she said.

"Yes, I am! I can't wait for the weekend."

"The week end?"

"Well, we've had three days of lessons, so I assume it must be Saturday soon. I need a break."

Lucy was surprised. "But today is Sunday," she said. "We have lessons every day, unless we have time off for some reason." She laughed at the look on Joe's face.

"You don't have weekends?" Joe groaned. "I don't know if I can keep this up."

"Come on! It's not that bad. Anyway, tomorrow is the start of a three day holiday."

Joe sat up again. "Thank heavens for that! Why?"

"There's going to be a feast, the day after tomorrow. Lots and lots of people are coming, so there are all the preparations to make."

"Oh yes." He frowned, vaguely. "Your mother said something about that. Do we have to help? Is that why we don't have lessons?"

"No, but the slaves who teach us are needed for other duties."

Joe yawned again.

"You need to get an early night, tonight," Lucy said. "Then we can do something together in the morning."

By the time they'd finished supper, however, it didn't feel all that early. Joe trudged off to his room. He felt exhausted. How did Petrus manage? Perhaps it was something you got used to. Part way through this thought, he fell asleep.

He was woken the next morning by Arethusa shaking him.

"Goodness me, Master Valentinian! You are a heavy sleeper!"

"Isn't it a holiday today?" Joe said blearily.

"For you, perhaps."

"Can't I have a lie-in, then?"

"You mean stay in bed to sleep? Oh, no, Master Valentinian! That wouldn't do at all." She bustled out.

Joe sat up. He ached all over.

There was a knock on the door. "Come in!"

Lucy stood in the doorway. "Aren't you going to get up?"

Joe threw himself back on his bed. "I don't want to."

She shook her head. "You can't just give up!"

"You don't know what it's like!" he protested. "You don't have to do any of the things we're doing with Heraclio."

"No." Lucy looked wistful.

"It's alright for you! Bits of me hurt that I never knew existed. You have it easy!"

"Do I?"

Joe sat up and pulled his nightshirt off over his head. When he looked at Lucy again, she was fiddling with the bulla at the neck of her dress.

"You know, sometimes I'd like to do those things," she said. "Ride, swim, use a sword."

"Why don't you, then?"

She frowned. "Girls don't."

"But you're rich! Why can't you just tell your parents you want to do it? There are so many slaves, there must be someone who could teach you if Heraclio doesn't have time. Or you could join me and Petrus." He pulled his shirt on.

Lucy pushed the bulla back down inside her dress. "It's not like that." Her voice was choked. "You don't get it, do you? Girls do weaving, boys do fighting. That's how it is." She turned on her heel. "I'm going for breakfast," she said over her shoulder. "See you there."

Joe thought about what she'd said while he finished getting dressed. At home, if you wanted to learn horse riding or swimming, it was down to whether your parents had enough money. He'd never thought about what it might be like to have your choices limited by whether you were a boy or a girl.

In the dining room, Lucy was sitting with her sisters on one of the couches. She didn't look up as he came in. Joe wondered if he needed to say sorry, but he wasn't quite sure what for. Sorry that things are different here from back at home? Or perhaps, sorry I didn't understand? Neither of those really made sense. He helped himself to fruit and sat down on the couch opposite.

The girls talked quietly among themselves for a couple of minutes. Joe wondered if Lucy was deliberately keeping her voice down so that he couldn't hear what she was saying. Then Sallustia stood up.

"See you in there," she said to Lucy and Antonia. Then to Joe, as an afterthought, "See you later, Valentinian."

"See you in where?" he asked, after she'd gone.

"The baths," Lucy said. "It's part of getting ready for tomorrow."

"I can't come with you, can I?"

Antonia giggled, but Lucy was stern. "Of course not! You go after the midday meal."

"I thought we were going to do something together this morning?" Joe knew he sounded like a little child.

Lucy shrugged. "I'd forgotten about the baths. There should still be time, maybe after I come out, or after you've finished this afternoon. Come on, Antonia. Let's go."

Joe finished his breakfast alone. He felt fed up. He'd been looking forward to spending the day with Lucy. But first he'd managed to upset her, and now she was busy for the morning, and he would be at the baths for the afternoon.

He left the dining room and wandered out into the colonnades to see what was going on. There were usually quite a number of different tasks being done when he walked to his classes with Petrus, but today there were fewer slaves sitting at their carving or mending, and far more hurrying to and fro.

Women trotted past with vast baskets of linen, and trays of plates, bowls, and jugs. In the formal gardens, four men rather than one were clipping the hedges, and a further four were scrubbing the statues and fountains to remove any trace of green. Along the north colonnade, there were huge piles of foliage and flowers being made into enormous garlands. A ship must have come in the previous day as well, because there was a steady stream of men carrying crates from the direction of the shore over towards the north side of the compound.

While Joe watched, a group of ten men staggered past carrying a very large crate covered with a cloth. They were heading towards the hall at the eastern end of the north wing. Joe's attention was caught by a strange noise that came from the crate from time to time, somewhere between a yowl and a snarl. Each time it happened, the crate lurched one way or the other, and the men lurched with it, struggling to hold it steady.

He was so absorbed in wondering what might be beneath the cloth that he didn't see Tiberius until it was too late.

"Watching people at work again?" Tiberius sneered. "That's a favourite pastime of yours, isn't it!"

Joe said nothing.

"Maybe you should try working a bit yourself! I hear you're not doing too well at your lessons."

Joe shot him a look.

"It's hardly a secret, is it?" Tiberius swaggered. "Master Valentinian seems not to have had any schooling, they say. He doesn't know how to handle a sword or ride a horse, even though he's the son of a General. And they're surprised!" He smiled, but there was no pleasure in his face.

Joe turned more calmly than he felt, and walked away.

But Tiberius fell into step beside him, as though they were having a friendly chat. "Tell me, do you agree that they would be even more surprised to know that you're not the son of a General?"

Joe could feel his heart beating fast. If Tiberius had been afraid of him before, he wasn't now.

"Who am I then?" He tried to sound brave. As long as they were surrounded by people, Tiberius probably wouldn't hurt him. Joe wondered what to do when they came to the end of the east colonnade. There was such a stream of people scurrying in and out of the hall at the north east corner that he would have to stop.

"I'm not sure it matters who you are," Tiberius said. "What I do know is that someone has helped you to pass yourself off as somebody you're not!" He caught hold of Joe's wrist. His grip was strong.

"The question is, who? There's Lucilia, of course, your Lucy." In a sudden flick, he twisted Joe's arm behind his back.

Pain shot up through Joe's shoulder. He gasped.

"I could see if she'd like to tell me anything," Tiberius hissed in his ear.

"No!" The word flew out of Joe's mouth. He pressed his lips together. "She doesn't know who I am. It's nothing to do with her."

"I don't agree," said Tiberius pleasantly, not letting go. "Whatever lies you've told to Helena Calvina, you've had help from little Lucy. The story, for one thing. That's hers, isn't it? But it isn't just her, is it?" He twisted Joe's arm harder.

Joe cried out. Two slaves nearby glanced up, then instantly looked away again.

Tiberius held Joe's wrist a few seconds longer, then dropped it.

His arm fell back to his side. The blood coursed into it again. But before he could feel relief, the older boy grabbed a handful of his hair.

"There's this too, isn't there?" he jeered. "You were blond last time you were here."

Joe's eyes watered. He felt as though his hair was being yanked out. He stumbled towards Tiberius. The world around him blurred. He heard a whispering in his ears.

"No!" He shouted. "Not yet!" He clenched his teeth. He would not leave Lucy yet.

"Not yet what?" Tiberius let go of his hair.

Joe reeled away, dizzy. "I'm not ready," he muttered to himself through his teeth.

Tiberius sprang away. "Ready? For what?"

Joe looked up.

The world snapped into sharp focus. There was alarm in Tiberius' face. Joe narrowed his eyes. For some reason, this boy, who was older and bigger than Joe, was suddenly afraid of him.

Joe knew he had to seize his chance. He advanced on Tiberius.

"What do you think I am?" he said in a low voice. "Have you any idea what I can do?"

Tiberius backed away.

"You don't know, do you! You think I really can't ride a horse? You think I really can't use a sword? You believe that?"

Tiberius was pale. "I don't know what to believe!" he stammered, still edging away.

"If people only knew what I can do ..." Joe fixed his eyes on Tiberius' face. "Perhaps I should show them. Perhaps I should start with you, since you're the one causing me all the trouble." He kept walking slowly towards Tiberius.

The other boy glanced over his shoulder.

Rage made Joe feel invincible, but he knew that he couldn't carry out his own threat. He had to scare Tiberius away.

The older boy looked over his shoulder again. "Leave me alone!" he hissed.

Joe glared at Tiberius. "Then you leave me alone!" he said savagely.

For a moment, Tiberius' mouth contorted

strangely. Then he spat at the ground directly in front of Joe, a huge, bubbling pool of saliva.

On instinct, Joe stepped forward and smeared it deliberately across the ground beneath his foot. Tiberius stared, then whirled round and disappeared away down the colonnade.

Joe sat down on the wall between two pillars, and waited for his heart to stop pounding.

All around him, the slaves carried on with their tasks. Joe watched them as they passed. Not one of them looked at him. He might as well have been invisible.

He shivered. He'd thought he was safe as long as he was in a busy place. But Tiberius could have beaten him bloody in front of all these people, and not one of them would done anything to stop it.

He rubbed his hands up and down his arms to warm them. When he was first here, that would have outraged him. But he was starting to understand the way things worked. It would be much too risky for a slave to admit even seeing anything. Tiberius wouldn't hesitate to have them punished. For the first time, Joe felt worried for Arethusa and the scribe, Septimus. In helping him, they had put themselves in great danger.

He shuddered and got to his feet. So far in Lucy's world, he hadn't encountered the grisliness and bloodshed that was in every book he'd read about the Romans. But all at once, he had a strong feeling that if he only scratched the surface of life here, the violence would be there, instantly, like the blood that fills a cut.

11

Joe kept away from the palace buildings for the rest of the morning. He was fairly sure that Tiberius wouldn't pick on him again, at least for a day or two, but he was too worn out to make conversation with anyone else.

Lucy didn't emerge from the baths until midday, and then she was unusually quiet. Joe wondered if she was still cross with him. But she'd never stayed cross for more than a few seconds before, and she wasn't unfriendly, just wrapped up in her own thoughts.

After they'd eaten their midday meal, he decided to go to the bath house immediately himself, since Lucy wasn't in the mood to go and do anything. He could have waited for Petrus to finish whatever he was doing. But this was one of the only day-to-day experiences left where everyone would assume that he knew what to do, and he didn't want to have to hide his ignorance from Lucy's brother.

He ought to be able to manage on his own, he

thought, as long as nobody was watching him too carefully. After the experience he'd had, going to the loo when he was first here, he'd made sure that he looked at the descriptions of bathing while he was back at home. And even though the books didn't seem to agree on the order for using the different rooms of the bath house, he had a fair idea what to expect.

As he took off his clothes in the changing area, he thought of himself reading about this last week. It seemed so far away, as though it had been a different life.

It was weird to imagine Sam still asleep on the sofa-bed in Dad's sitting room. Was his own body also there, he wondered, lying next to his brother? What would happen if Dad came into the room and woke them? Would he be hauled back into his own time? But Dad just walking into the room would take a number of seconds, and if this was like last time, he shouldn't be away even for that long.

Abruptly, he felt worried. What if the time thing worked differently to how he'd thought? He'd been assuming that time stood still at home while he was here. But what if there was some kind of ratio between Lucy's time and his own? What if each of Lucy's hours was a second in his own time?

When he was here in Lucy's world before, it had been for less than twenty-four hours. He could easily have been away from his own world for twenty-four seconds without knowing. But he'd been here now for four nights and five days. How many hours was that? How many seconds of absence? It could be enough that his dad might notice if he came into the sitting room. And then what exactly *would* he notice? That Joe wasn't there? Or that he didn't respond to anything around him? At least it was still night time, he hoped.

In any case, there was nothing to be done about it at the moment. He took off his underclothes and made himself concentrate on what he was doing. According to all the books, the Romans went into the baths naked. But even though there was nobody around, he felt uncomfortable wearing nothing at all. At the end of the room, he spied some shelves of towels. Gratefully, he took one and wrapped it round his waist.

There were wooden sandals on a rack beneath. He didn't remember anything about those from the books, but he took a pair anyway. They were hard, and didn't really fit on his feet. When he walked, they clopped against the floor.

He wondered whether he'd been wrong to come without Petrus. He'd assumed that there would be someone here already that he could watch, to see what he was supposed to do. But the place was empty. Of course, if the slaves didn't use the baths, which he supposed they probably didn't, there couldn't be all that many men in the palace who would come here.

Still, if there was nobody else around, it didn't matter that there was no-one to copy, because there was no-one to see if he got it all wrong either.

He went through to the first room. It was small, cold, and dark, lit only by the daylight that filtered in through two small windows below the domed ceiling. He found that he was surprised.

He shook his head at himself. He should be used to indoor darkness by now. Every room in the palace was darker than rooms at home, because the windows were always so small and dirty, and there was no electric light. But of course all the pictures he'd seen of baths were either drawings in which everything was nice and bright, or photographs of ruins, where the roof or some of the walls had disappeared.

He looked around. There were alcoves in the walls on either side, where he imagined you might sit if you wanted to be in cool darkness. Set in the floor directly in front of him was a circular pool carved in stone, with a step all the way round.

Joe kicked off his sandals and unwrapped the towel. He wasn't sure whether he was supposed to go right into the water, so he sat down on the edge of the pool and dipped his feet in. It was icy. He winced. There was no way he was going to get right in, even if that was what you were supposed to do. He made himself hold his feet in the water, and gritted his teeth while he splashed his body all over. This was horrible! He huddled the towel around his body, shuffled into his sandals, and went through to the next room.

This one was much bigger, and had a large

square pool in the middle. It was lighter too, with more windows and candlelight flickering on the walls. Best of all, it was warm.

Joe breathed a sigh of relief as he stepped down into the pool and let himself slide backwards into the water. It was like having a hot bath in something the size of a swimming pool. He allowed himself to swoosh lazily around, watching the steam rise from the surface of the water.

"There you are!"

Joe flipped round towards the voice. It was Petrus.

"I thought I might find you here. Have you been in the caldarium?"

Joe paddled himself into an upright position, flustered by the question. Which was the caldarium? He watched Petrus' face for a clue. The other boy's eyes flicked towards a room he hadn't been into.

"No, not yet," he said, as coolly as he could.

"We usually go in there before we bathe."

"Oh. I see." Joe thought perhaps he'd better apologise. "Sorry."

"Never mind." Petrus nodded towards the doorway. "Come on. We'll come back in here in a bit."

Reluctantly, Joe swam to the side of the pool and got out. He felt self-conscious that he wasn't wearing anything, but Petrus didn't seem bothered.

The room they went into was dark and roasting hot. Joe kicked off his sandals. The soles of his feet smarted against the burning hot floor. He scuffed the sandals hastily back on, struggling all the while for breath. The air was somehow incredibly thick. It pressed against his chest.

Petrus poured water from a jug on to a bank of tiles at the end of the room. Steam filled the air. It felt like a knife at the back of Joe's throat. He wheezed and coughed.

"The laconium is next door. Would you prefer that?" Petrus asked.

"Yes, please," croaked Joe. He couldn't remember what the laconium involved, but it had to be better than this.

The room next door was similarly hot and dark, and barely bigger than a cupboard. Joe kept his sandals on this time and took shallow breaths. But although the heat was intense, it was dry and didn't hurt his throat as it had done in the steam room.

He and Petrus sat silently side by side on their towels on the stone bench. He felt sweat breaking out all over his body.

"That's enough," Petrus said, after a few minutes. "It's not good to stay too long."

Back in the room with the warm pool, he took a bottle from a shelf and poured something into the palm of his hand. "Here," he said, holding out the bottle.

Joe recognised the smell. It was olive oil. He copied Petrus, dipping his fingertips in his palm and rubbing the oil over his skin.

"It's always surprising how cool it feels out here, after the hot rooms," Petrus said.

Joe nodded.

Petrus took two pieces of metal from a basket on the shelf. "Have a strigil," he said, handing one of them to Joe.

Joe took it nonchalantly, as he had done the wax tablet and stylus when they'd had their first lesson together. It still seemed strange, actually using the kinds of objects he'd only seen behind the glass of museum cases.

This one was a kind of half hook, where the curved end had been beaten flat like the blade of a knife. Joe imitated Petrus, using the edge of his blade to scrape his skin where he'd oiled it. The sensation was surprisingly pleasant, and despite plastering himself with oil, he did feel cleaner too.

"Let's bathe," Petrus said, when they'd finished. He put the strigils back in the basket and took a running jump into the pool, curling his legs up and wrapping his arms around them.

Joe hooted with laughter. "No bombing!" he shouted, as Petrus surfaced.

"No what?"

"Never mind." Joe jumped into the pool. He hadn't slipped up by saying anything as un-Roman as that the whole time he'd been here. He swam under the water as far as he could before he bobbed up. Petrus was standing on the side, about to jump in again.

"I didn't think you were allowed to jump in like that," Joe said.

Petrus grinned. "Not in public baths, and not if there was anyone else here. But who's going to know?" He spread his arms wide in a grand shrug, then dived into the water.

They didn't get out until nearly supper time. On their way back through the frigidarium, Petrus said, "One last thing - a quick dip in here. It's good for you!"

He plunged in to the cold pool. "Owww! That is freezing!" he howled. He pulled himself out on to the side, panting. "Your turn!"

Joe took a deep breath and jumped in. The cold hit him like a rock. He felt his limbs spasm. His brain seemed to empty. Everything went dark. It was very quiet. This is it, he thought. Either I'm going to die, or I'm going to be pulled back home, right in front of Petrus.

But the next thing he knew, Petrus was dragging him up on to the side. "Are you alright?" His face was white. "You stopped moving. I thought you'd ... I don't know, I thought you'd ..." He couldn't finish the sentence.

Joe rolled over on the floor. It was cold, but nothing like as cold as the water. "It's fine," he mumbled. "I thought I was going. But I'm fine." His teeth started to chatter.

Petrus threw a towel over him. "Come on, let's

get dressed. You need to get warm."

But Joe was still shivering when they left the bath house.

"I'm sorry," Petrus said. "I shouldn't have made you do that."

"Never mind," Joe said, trying to hold his jaw steady while he spoke. "I'll be okay."

"Okay?"

"I'll be alright." Quite suddenly, another wave of homesickness swept over Joe. It was too much, keeping up the pretence, remembering not to say 'okay', trying all the time to guess what would happen next so that he didn't put his foot in it.

He couldn't imagine ever being warm again either. If he were at home, Mum would give him extra jumpers and tuck him up under a duvet with a hot water bottle.

He turned his head away so that Petrus wouldn't see him blinking back tears.

The hollow in the pit of his stomach continued most of the way through supper. Joe ate what he could but said nothing. As the food started at last to warm him up, he noticed that nobody else was speaking much either.

He tried to catch Lucy's eye, but she didn't lift her gaze from her plate. Sallustia stared at the floor and ate nothing at all, while Antonia sat between them, glancing anxiously back and forth. The boys talked a little, and Lucy's father made a pronouncement from time to time. Lucy's mother gazed into the distance and didn't reply.

When the children were finally allowed to leave the room, Joe caught Lucy's sleeve as she walked out.

"What's the matter?" he whispered. "What's going on?"

She looked up at him. The expression on her face was bleak. "Sorry, Joe. I didn't realise today would be like this."

Joe looked round quickly to see if anyone had heard her say his real name, but there was no-one close by. Lucy seemed completely unaware.

"It's Sallustia," she said. "The feast, tomorrow. It's to celebrate her marriage."

Joe frowned. "I thought you said nothing had been arranged for her."

"It hadn't," Lucy said. "But there was a betrothal agreed while our cousins were here in August. I didn't know." She hung her head.

"Is she marrying one of your cousins, then?"

"No, the stepson of one of my uncles."

"Is it really that bad?"

She nodded.

"Why?"

"Oh, Joe." Lucy flung her arms around his neck and buried her face in his shoulder. "He's awful," she sobbed. "He's horribly ugly - he has these nasty pustules all over his face! I know he can't help it, but you don't even want to look at him! But worse than that, he's really mean, like Tiberius, only even nastier." She wailed.

Joe patted her awkwardly on the back. "Why does Sallustia have to marry him? Couldn't they find someone else? After all, she's pretty and nice and well educated, as well as your father's daughter."

"That's just it!" Lucy let go of him and wiped her eyes with her sleeve. "It's a political match. His father was a senator in Rome, and his mother is from one of the great families of Rome. It makes sense." She sniffed and swallowed another sob.

"What does Sallustia think?"

"She hates him!"

"Doesn't that count for something?"

Lucy shook her head. Her eyes brimmed over again with tears. "Nobody cares what Sallustia wants. This is what she has to do. That's how it is!" She covered her face with her hands. "It's so unfair! Oh Joe, it's so unfair!" Her voice rose in a wail. "I've been thinking all day how I don't want to be here! I don't want to see Sallustia marry him!" Her shoulders shook.

Joe put his arms cautiously around her.

"I want to go away from here," she sobbed. "I want to go to wherever it is you come from. I want to come and live with you!"

12

When Joe woke up the next morning, he wasn't sure whether he was still glad to be in Lucy's world. On other days, he'd woken up with a feeling of excitement. But when he'd left Lucy last night, she was still so tearful at the prospect of Sallustia's wedding feast that he wasn't really looking forward to it either. As he got dressed, he found himself wishing that he at least knew how much longer he was going to be staying here.

Lucy looked tired but composed at breakfast. There was nobody else there, but he didn't know whether they'd already eaten or not yet come down.

"Are you alright?" he asked, sitting down on the couch next to her.

"Yes, thank you." She pressed her lips together. "Please don't be too nice to me though, or I might cry again."

"Right." Joe frowned. Girls were strange. Why would someone being nice to you make you cry? "So," he said, "what do we do now?"

She pushed her fruit around her plate but didn't eat much of it. "We can do something together after breakfast," she said, without enthusiasm. "Then after our midday meal, we get into our best clothes ready for the feast."

Joe looked down at himself. "I don't have any best clothes."

"Never mind. Arethusa will find you something."

"And do you ..." Joe hesitated, afraid to mention Sallustia in case he started Lucy off crying again. "Do you need to do anything with your sister?"

"No." Lucy looked at her feet. "She'll be with my mother and her lady's maids, getting ready."

"What, all day?"

"Most of it. I suppose this is the time when my mother tells her the things she needs to know." She pulled a face.

"Like what?" Joe asked blankly.

"How to please her husband, that kind of thing."

They looked at each other.

Joe wrinkled his nose. "Yuck!"

Lucy laughed. Joe felt a bubble of happiness rise in his chest at the sound of it. Lucy was the reason he most liked being here, but he hadn't seen enough of her over the last few days.

Almost at once, her shoulders drooped again. He tried to think of a way of cheering her up. Suddenly, he remembered what he'd seen yesterday. "The feast is going to be in the hall at the end of the north wing, isn't it?"

"That's right."

"I saw something interesting being carried in there yesterday morning. Let's go and have a look."

"What was it?"

"I don't know. There was a very large box under a cloth, but I swear it was making a strange noise."

Lucy brightened at once. "How exciting!"

They went back around the south wing and along the east colonnade. Slaves scurried past them, intent on their tasks. Joe could feel a flutter of anticipation in his stomach.

The hall they stepped into was every bit as impressive as the entrance hall in the east wing, and it had been lavishly decorated. Half way down the left hand side was a platform with six throne-like seats beneath an archway of roses; at either end of this were two great pyramids of tall white candles; and all the way down the room, the pillars which supported the roof had been encircled with garlands of leaves and flowers.

"What's that?" Lucy whispered.

Down at the far end, mounted on a pedestal, was a large golden cage like an ornamental birdcage. Something lay on the floor of it.

Joe caught his breath.

"What is it?" Lucy whispered again, as they

tiptoed towards it.

The animal's ear twitched.

"It's a leopard," Joe murmured.

"What's one of those?"

"One of the big cats. They hunt across the great plains of Africa."

"What do you think?" a voice boomed behind them.

Joe and Lucy both jumped. The leopard's eyes flicked open and it raised its head, immediately wary.

"Isn't it beautiful?" Lucullus strode down the hall towards them. "It's called a leopard. Have you ever seen anything like it?"

Joe bit his tongue to stop himself from giving an honest answer.

"It's a gift to our house from Sallustia's new family in Rome," Lucullus went on. "It's to celebrate the wedding."

The animal growled as he approached. It was crouching now, its muscles taut, its tail swishing slowly from side to side.

"Be calm, you beautiful creature," Lucullus said in a soothing tone. "We won't hurt you. The slave will bring you meat very soon."

Again the leopard growled.

"She's wild, isn't she?" Lucullus said with admiration. "I expect she'd like to be free to roam, but she's too dangerous."

"What will you do with her, father?"

Lucullus looked thoughtfully at Lucy. "She'll have to stay in her cage for the feast. After that, we'll see. She shouldn't really be here, though she's a lovely gift." He put his hand on his daughter's shoulder and looked at the leopard for a few moments. The leopard looked back at him, its great amber eyes scarcely blinking.

"Now then," Lucullus said. "It's time to go to the lararium." He turned and strode out.

"What's a lararium?" Joe whispered as they followed him.

"It's the shrine," Lucy said. "He makes offerings to the household gods every few days. But on special days, we all go."

The shrine was in the entrance hall of the east wing. Joe hadn't noticed it as he hurried through before. It was a little bit like a puppet theatre built in stone, he thought, with pillars to either side and a roof above. Three figures were painted on the wall at the back, where the scenery would be, and beneath them was painted an enormous snake.

Lucy's father bent to add a bunch of grapes and a jug of wine to the flowers which already lay on the shrine. Lucy and Joe joined the rest of the family at a respectful distance behind him.

"On this, the occasion of our daughter's marriage," he was saying, "we ask that our guests may feel welcome and well provided for."

Joe glanced at Sallustia. Her dark hair was

wound elaborately on top of her head and studded with gems. Beneath it, her face showed no emotion.

"... and we ask that this house may continue to prosper." Lucy's father dropped down on one knee and bowed his head in prayer. Then he stood up and spread his arms wide. "We shall give the greatest feast this family has ever seen!" he said grandly.

After that, time seemed to speed up. Lucy and Joe wandered down to the shore and back, but then it was time for the midday meal. As soon as they'd finished that, they were sent off to get ready.

Joe washed and changed into the clothes Arethusa had laid out for him, and then went to see if Lucy and Antonia had finished their preparations. But the two girls still sat in their petticoats with their hair piled up like Sallustia's and decorated with flowers, while the ladies' maids hurried in and out bringing dresses and jewellery.

Outside, Joe could hear the sound of rising chatter. He went out to see what was happening.

The colonnades were already busy with guests. It struck Joe that the men looked like something out of one of his library books. It must be because they were wearing togas. Previously, all the men he'd seen had worn tunics like his own. He hadn't thought about that before.

Among the white of the togas, the women's robes were vivid: purple, blue, red and orange. The air was scented with the fragrance of sandalwood and lavender.

He watched quietly, people talking and laughing, preening and strutting. As more and more arrived, a kind of circular procession began, from the entrance in the east wing, up the path in the middle of the formal gardens, along the front of the west wing, and back down the north colonnade to the banqueting hall.

"Look at her," Lucy whispered beside Joe.

He turned. "Wow! You look really pretty!" he exclaimed, and then immediately blushed.

Lucy turned pink too. "Thank you," she said shyly. "But I was looking at that." She pointed to an exotic bird mounted in a woman's hair. "Is it alive, do you think?"

"It can't be. It would be flapping its wings."

Another woman passed with peacock feathers trailing over the back of her skirt.

"It looks just like the real thing," Lucy breathed.

"Do you think she's got a string she pulls to fan them out behind her head?" Joe whispered. They burst into fits of giggles.

"Look at him!" Lucy said when she'd stopped laughing, nodding towards one of the men. "I didn't know it was possible to be that fat!"

"And what about her?" Joe replied, pointing at a haughty looking woman. "You wouldn't mess with her!"

"I wish they'd hurry up," Lucy said.

"Where have they all come from?" Joe asked.

"All over the country, and from abroad too, some of them."

Finally, the flow of people dwindled. "Time to go," Lucy said.

Joe looked across the now empty gardens. Marius, Petrus and Antonia were already waiting at the end of the north colonnade, at the entrance to the banqueting hall. They joined them, and watched Lucullus and Helena Calvina walk round from the south wing. There was no sign of Tiberius, but from the north wing, another couple emerged, followed by a young man.

"That's my uncle and his new wife," Lucy whispered. "And there's her horrible son."

"Where's Sallustia?"

"She comes later, when the ceremony is about to begin." Lucy shivered.

The noise inside the hall was suddenly hushed. As Lucullus stepped into the building, cheering and applause erupted. Lucy's parents and Sallustia's new husband and parents made their way through the throng of guests and up on to the platform. The crowd surged around them, as people pressed forward to pay their respects to their host.

"Do you have to go up there too?" Joe nodded to the line of thrones.

"No, thank goodness," Lucy said. "We can enjoy ourselves a bit, at least until the ceremony." She grimaced.

Joe looked around. The hall was bright with the light from the pyramids of candles beside the platform, and from candelabras on the walls all the way down the room. "This is amazing!"

"You wait till the food comes!" Lucy grinned. "There should be fattened snails again - remember how much you liked those last time? And probably dormouse pies and peacock eggs. If we're lucky, there might even be a roasted boar filled with live birds. It's alright," she said quickly. "They just fly out and straight up to the rafters."

A slave passed by with a tray of silver cups, and handed one to each of them.

Joe sniffed his. "What's this?" he asked doubtfully.

"Wine and water for the children." Lucy raised her cup to him. "Bene tibi!" she said.

Joe did the same. "Bene tibi!" He took a sip. "Ugh! It tastes like vinegar!"

Lucy drew herself up. "That's my father's best wine you're talking about!" she said indignantly. But Joe could see her trying not to pull a face as she drank from her own cup. "Oh, by the way, there's something I have to tell you," she said. Her cheeks were slightly pink again. "Promise you won't be cross with me?"

Joe looked at her, puzzled. "Yes, I promise. But what on earth have you done that might make me cross?"

She put her hand to her throat, and reached down inside the neck of her dress. "I found this." Between her finger and thumb, she held his St. Christopher, hung on a fine leather cord.

He stared at it. "Why didn't you tell me before? I mean, it's good that you found it. I didn't know if it was actually here. But why didn't you say?"

Lucy looked down into her cup. "I thought it might have something to do with calling you back. I was touching it just before you appeared again, and I thought maybe there was some magic to it, or something."

Joe laughed. "That's daft! How could there be?"

Lucy stuck out her chin belligerently. "How else did you get here, then?"

"I don't know," he admitted. "I thought it was because I was thinking of you at the same moment as you were thinking of me."

"It might have been that too, but I touched it, and there you were." She let it hang on its cord against the front of her dress. "Anyway, I thought if you knew I had it, you'd want it back. And then I wouldn't be able to call you if I needed you."

Joe thought about this. "I would like it back in the end," he said. "It was a present from my dad. But you can keep it for now."

All at once, Lucy seized the St. Christopher and stuffed it back inside the neck of her dress, spilling her drink in her haste.

"It's alright!" Joe laughed. "I wasn't going to grab it from you!"

"Grab what?" asked a voice behind him.

Joe swung round.

Tiberius stood there, his lip curled in a sneer. "What has she got that you might want?"

"Nothing." Joe felt himself flush.

"Really?" Tiberius leaned towards him, as though he was about to share a secret. "The trouble with you is that every time I talk to you, I get the feeling you're lying." He smiled sweetly.

"Just go away, Tiberius!" Lucy said. Her eyes flashed. "Why can't you leave us alone?"

Tiberius stepped back and put his hands up in front of him. "No need to get all hot and bothered. I was just coming to give you a tip off." He looked at Joe. "Your parents are here. I thought you'd like to know."

"My parents ...?" For a moment, Joe thought he meant Mum and Dad. "But they're ..."

"Well, I say 'your parents'. I mean the people who are supposed to be your parents, according to your story."

Joe looked at Lucy. Her face was white.

"That's right, little Lucy," Tiberius said, in a voice heavy with sarcasm. "Marcus Placidius is here with his wife Severina Orbiana." He turned to Joe. "They don't seem to have brought the children, but I'm sure they'd be pleased to meet you instead!" He turned and disappeared into the crowd.

"Oh, Lucy!" Joe groaned. "I've been so stupid! I should have known! Your mother said something about Severina Orbiana coming to this feast when I went to see her. I didn't know what she meant at the time, and then I forgot all about it." He scanned the queue of people waiting to pay their respects to Lucullus and Helena Calvina. But it was no use. He had no idea who he was looking for.

"What are we going to do?" asked Lucy desperately.

Joe chewed his thumbnail. "I don't know. Create a distraction somehow?"

"But how?"

Before he could answer, an unearthly yowl filled the hall. For a split second, there was silence. Then people began to scream.

On instinct, Joe pulled Lucy towards him, back against the wall. A moment later, there was a tidal wave in the crowd. The guests who had been standing at the end of the hall began to run towards the entrance, pushing others in front of them. Joe felt his toes crushed under a man's foot as he lurched past them.

"It's the leopard!" someone yelled. "The leopard's out!"

"Get the guards!"

Pandemonium broke out all over the hall. The screaming rose in pitch. People pushed and staggered. They slipped and tripped. They fell and trampled each other in their rush to escape.

Pinned against the wall, Joe saw a flurry of skirts, open mouths, arms and legs, terrified eyes. Beneath the shouting and the thunder of feet, he seemed to hear the snarling of the cornered animal.

But it wasn't so much snarling as hissing. The screaming died away, though the mouths were still open. The room seemed to fade in and out. Joe blinked.

"Help me!" He caught hold of Lucy's wrist.

"What's the matter?" Her face was tight with terror.

"I'm going ..." He struggled to speak. "I think ... I'm about to disappear!"

"In there!" She pushed him away from her, behind a heavy curtain which hung down beside them. But even as he slipped into it, Joe felt his grip on her wrist loosening. The gold thread of the fabric stopped shining. The chaos in the hall was muffled. He was in darkness. He felt dizzy.

He reached out to steady himself. The curtain was gone. The shouting and screaming had stopped, and the stampeding of a thousand feet had become the rumble of passing traffic. He was sitting up in bed in Dad's flat.

He touched his own face, the bedclothes, his pyjamas. Then he threw himself back on the bed, and let relief pour over him.

13

Joe woke the next morning from the deepest sleep he could ever remember.

"Come on, lazy bones!" Sam booted the end of the sofa-bed.

"How long have you been up?" Joe mumbled.

"Over an hour. We haven't been creeping around either. I can't believe you didn't wake up!"

Joe drifted through to the bathroom and began to clean his teeth, looking at himself vaguely in the mirror. It was only when he straightened up from rinsing the toothpaste away that he realised that he looked completely normal. It was just as well that his hair wasn't still black, but he was sorry he hadn't had the chance to see it. If the experience of having it dyed hadn't been so unpleasant, he would have thought he'd dreamt it. But there was no way his imagination could have conjured that smell.

He stood under the hot blast of the shower until Dad hammered on the bathroom door. "Get a move on,

Joe! We're going out in fifteen minutes."

"Where are we going?" Joe asked, as he pulled on his clothes and went into the kitchen.

"It's Sam's choice today, so it's Laser Quest."

"Do we have to?"

"Yes, we do," Dad said. "We went to Fishbourne yesterday, didn't we, even though Sam didn't want to."

"I suppose so." Joe helped himself to breakfast. It seemed impossible that that was only yesterday. And what would Lucy think of today's activity, him and Sam leaping around in the dark, shooting each other with beams of light? Her life was so much more real.

With a sudden pit in his stomach, he realised he didn't know if she'd survived the leopard and the stampeding guests. She must have done, he decided. She couldn't have been killed. That would be too terrible. He put the thought determinedly out of his mind.

Laser Quest was fun after all, even though Joe couldn't shrug off the feeling that it was a weird thing to do. In a way, it was helpful too, because there was lots of time when he didn't have to talk to Dad or Sam. It seemed to be much more difficult to adjust to being back in his own world this time, after being away for so much longer.

What he really wanted was to get back to Dad's place, to the book Dad had bought him yesterday, so that he could read up about Lucy's father. The minute they got in, he went and fetched it and curled up on the sofa.

"If there are any bits you don't understand," Dad said, "just ask."

"It's fine." Joe turned to the index. Lucy's father wasn't in there. He frowned. Had the guide been wrong? He turned back to the contents page. And there it was, a whole chapter about him in chapter three. Joe flicked through to the right place in the book and began to read.

After a minute, he frowned again. A lot of the words were long, and they'd been strung together into difficult sentences. He scanned through for bits he could understand more easily. On the third page of the chapter was a paragraph set apart from the rest.

'The Emperor Domitian put many senators to death,' Joe read, *'including Sallustius Lucullus, governor of Britain.'*

"Oh no!" he gasped. He read the rest of the section. There was no mistake. Lucy's father had been killed by the Emperor.

"What's the matter?" Dad looked up from his cup of tea.

Joe stared at him, unable to think what to say. Lucy's father had been put to death. Executed. That was like Dad being executed. In fact, it was like Dad being executed by the queen. It was ridiculous, but also horrifying.

"That man," he muttered, "the one who owned Fishbourne - the Emperor had him killed."

"Oh dear. What for?" Dad was completely unconcerned. But of course he would be. He didn't know this man or his family.

Joe looked down at the book. "Someone invented a new kind of lance, and it was named after him rather than the Emperor."

Dad smiled. "That sounds like a trumped up excuse, doesn't it? You can't imagine that was the real reason!"

Joe swallowed and put the book down. He had to hide how he felt, or Dad would think he was overreacting.

"We're lucky to live when we do," Dad said, sipping his tea. "I've thought that about most periods in history over the years."

"Mmmm." Joe got up. "I'm hungry," he lied, to change the subject.

That night, before he turned out the light, he picked up the book again. Although he was tired, he wanted to know everything he could find out about Lucy's father. But it didn't say where or how Lucullus had been executed, or even what year, only that it had been before AD96, because that was when the Emperor Domitian had died.

It was hopeless, Joe thought glumly. He didn't know what year it had been in Lucy's time anyway, and even if he'd asked her, he didn't know if she would be counting it the same way. Dates for the Romans were either BC, which he knew stood for 'Before

Christ' or AD, which meant afterwards, except the A wasn't for 'after'. But did Lucy even know about Jesus? She'd never said anything about religion, only about offerings to the household gods. Now that he thought about it, it seemed more than likely that the numbering system was something that historians had come up with later.

He put the book down and rolled over to try and sleep. There were just too many problems. As well as the dates, there was the leopard and the stampede, and the question of whether Lucy was okay. Then there was the same question as before, about whether he would be able to get back. And even if she was okay, and he *did* get back, there was now also the question of whether to tell her about what he'd found out.

If his own dad was going to die in a few years time, he didn't think he'd want to know, unless there was something he could do to change it. But Lucy wouldn't be able to change it, would she, even if he told her. Because if she did, the present would have to be changed as well. If she found a way to stop the Emperor from executing her father, the book that Dad had bought Joe would have to change so that it didn't say that any more. And since it was already printed, that had to be impossible.

He pulled the duvet up to his chin. Perhaps he shouldn't tell her, then. But in that case, he would have to try and act normally, and that would be really difficult, knowing what he knew. She was bound to notice, and if he didn't tell her what it was, or if he tried to lie, she would guess he was hiding something and get upset.

He groaned. His brain hurt.

The last couple of days with Dad passed pleasantly enough. Joe knew that he should be sad that their week together was coming to an end, but he was so preoccupied that he didn't think about it very much.

It was when he was unpacking his things back at home again that it really hit him. This was how it was going to be from now on: never any normal time with Mum and Dad together, and only bits of time at weekends and holidays with Dad.

He felt as though he'd wasted a lot of the last week, first wondering whether he would be able to get back into Lucy's time, and then worrying about her. It was stupid, he thought crossly. None of the stuff about Lucy mattered while he was still here in his own world.

So for the next few days, he tried not to think about her quite as much. In any event, he told himself, if she was right, and he'd been pulled into her world when she touched his St. Christopher, it was really up to her when she called him back. He could think about her all day long, but she was probably asleep for half the time, and even when they were both awake at the same time, she wouldn't ever touch the St. Christopher if there was anyone else nearby. On top of that, she had her own life, so she probably wasn't thinking about him all that often anyway. He had to get on with other things and stop mooning around, like he was waiting for her to call.

The question, though, was what to do. Mum had been extra nice since he and Sam got back, and kept asking if they wanted to invite friends round to play.

"I thought you might like to have people here," she said, "since I guess you went out a lot with Dad."

It was another one of her questions that was pretending not to be a question, Joe thought, like everything else she'd said about the time they'd spent with Dad. It reminded him of someone poking a bear with a stick. She sort of jabbed at the subject, jumping back each time. He couldn't work out whether she actually wanted to know what they'd done with Dad or not.

Sam invited Ben round straight away, but Joe refused. In spite of his efforts not to think about Lucy, she was the only person he wanted to see. He didn't know what he would talk to any of his other friends about.

The third time Mum asked, however, he said yes, to please her and to distract himself. But it was just as he'd feared. His friend, Matthew, joked around all afternoon, in a way that seemed childish to Joe, and they couldn't agree on anything to do together except for kicking a ball round the garden.

After Matthew had gone, Joe overheard Mum talking to Kate on the phone.

"I'm worried about him," she was saying. "He seems really badly affected by the separation, especially after staying with Steve for the week."

It isn't that! Joe wanted to shout from the top of the stairs. *I just want to be somewhere else!*

"The Roman obsession seems to have passed, though," said his mum. "He took his books back to the library and didn't borrow any others. Perhaps Steve bored him out of it!" She laughed. "He did buy him a really heavy book about Roman Sussex, not suitable for a ten year old at all."

It isn't an obsession! Joe shouted silently. *And it hasn't passed! Dad's book was really useful! I took the other books back because there's nothing new in them, now I've seen it all with my own eyes!*

He stomped into his room and banged the door. She would never understand. He threw himself down on his bed. He knew he was being unfair. How could she understand when he couldn't tell her any of it? But he wasn't in the mood to be fair.

"Come on, Lucy!" he said out loud. "Call me, please!" Nothing happened. He drummed on his pillow with his fists. "Come on!"

But for three more weeks, still nothing happened. Joe grew more and more irritable. Perhaps the adventure was over. Perhaps he never would go back to Lucy's time again. But he had such a strong feeling of unfinished business, he couldn't bear for this to be the end.

It was the last evening before he went back to school that it finally happened. He was standing in his room, looking at his uniform laid out on his bed, thinking about his lessons with Petrus, and wondering how Lucy and her brother were doing. And in the next moment, he had the same feeling he'd had before, of the world moving around him. There was the hissing sound, and suddenly he was in darkness.

He put out his hands and touched something slightly rough. He seemed to be wrapped in a column of material. Lucy had pushed him behind a curtain in the banqueting hall as he disappeared, so perhaps he'd reappeared in the same spot. It would be useful if that always happened, he thought.

He felt around until he found the edge of the curtain. All sound inside it was muffled, but he didn't think there was anybody on the other side. He wondered how much time had passed since he was last here. Cautiously, he drew back the curtain and stepped out.

Shafts of moonlight fell across the tiled floor from each of the high windows. The hall was otherwise in darkness. Joe looked around. There was nobody here and no sign of the feast. He glanced down at himself. He was wearing Roman clothes as usual.

Beside the curtain was a door. He tried it. It was locked. Further along the same wall was another door. The hall echoed with his footsteps. The second door was also locked.

He looked around again. The main entrance to the hall was closed off with a screen. Still, that seemed the most likely way out. He tiptoed across to it, looking over his shoulder every other second. But there was definitely nobody here to see him. At one side of the screen, there was a gap. Joe squeezed through it.

Outside, the formal gardens were bathed in moonlight so bright it was almost like day. The trees in the middle of each section of lawn cast sharp black shapes across the grass, and the floors of the colonnades were striped by the shadows of the pillars that held them up.

He wished he knew what time it was. It felt like the middle of the night, but it could be the early darkness of a winter evening. It was certainly much colder than when he was last here.

The thing to do was to find Lucy. She must have been thinking of him, to call him into her time, so even if it was the middle of the night, she must be awake.

Walking as smoothly and quietly as he could, he went down the east colonnade and along the south wing. The door to the servant rooms on the end of the building was closed. He went around to the side with the terraces. There were no candles lit in the courtyards, and no light visible in the rooms behind. He crept through the courtyard nearest to Lucy's room, and felt his way along the passage till he reached it.

Gently, he tapped on the door. There was no answer. He pushed it open and tiptoed in. His eyes had got used to the darkness as he crept along the passage, but still he rubbed them to try and see better. Lucy's bed stood in front of him. The covers were drawn up over it.

"Lucy," he whispered. He bent down and patted it with his hands, not wanting to believe what his eyes were telling him.

The bed was empty. Lucy was not there.

14

Joe stood in the darkness and wondered what to do. The palace was completely silent around him. If it was the middle of the night, as it seemed to be, then where on earth was Lucy?

Perhaps she'd got up to go to the loo, or to get a drink of water, he thought hopefully. But the covers of her bed were too neat. It hadn't been slept in. He felt panic rising in his chest. Perhaps she hadn't called him at all. Perhaps she'd been killed by the leopard or the stampede and he'd come back here some other way.

He sat down on her bed to try and calm himself. He thought back to the chaos that had broken out just before he disappeared last time. He didn't know whether Lucy's parents had found out that he wasn't really Valentinian. He didn't know whether they'd noticed he'd gone, or what they thought about it, or what Lucy had said. Tiberius was sure to have said his piece once Joe was safely out of the way. He shivered.

"Where are you, Lucy?" he whispered.

There was no reply.

He stood up. He couldn't stay here. Someone might come in, if not during the night then tomorrow morning. But until he'd found Lucy, assuming she was still here somewhere, he couldn't risk being seen at all. He would have to hide.

He tried to think where to go. It was too cold outside to hide in the shrubbery where Arethusa had dyed his hair. And it was too risky to go back to the room he'd stayed in last time he was here. He thought about the other areas of the palace. Nowhere seemed safe. Then he had an idea. The one place where he was unlikely to be discovered was Arethusa's linen cupboard, where he'd slept the first time he was here.

He tiptoed out of Lucy's room and crept through the passageways until he found it. Inside, it was pitch black. Arethusa had put an oil lamp in here before, as well as a mattress. At the time, it hadn't seemed very comfortable, but it would be even less comfortable now.

He lifted a stack of sheets from the racks and put them down in a pile on the bare floor beside the wall. "Sorry, Arethusa," he muttered. "I'll try not to get them too dirty." He sat down on top of them. They made a rather hard seat, but it was better than sitting directly on the floor. He closed his eyes and leaned back against the wall.

He wasn't aware of falling asleep, but he was jolted awake by a scream which was instantly cut short. His eyes flew open. Arethusa stood in the doorway, her hand clamped over her mouth. Her eyes were wide with horror, as though she'd seen a monster.

"It's okay, Arethusa," Joe said. "It's only me!" But as he went to stand up, she backed away from him. "What's the matter? Don't you recognise me? It's Joe, or Valentinian. Remember?"

She took her hand away from her mouth. "I don't know who or what you are," she whimpered. "But I don't want anything to do with you!"

Joe took a step towards her. "Please, Arethusa! Don't be scared." He reached out and caught her sleeve. "No, don't go, please!"

Arethusa cowered away from him.

"You know I won't hurt you. What are you so frightened of?"

"You're a spirit," she whispered. "That's what they said. You appear from nowhere, make trouble, and then disappear again."

"I know it might seem like that. But I'm not. Truly, I'm not! And anyway, how did I make trouble?"

"Well, there was the leopard for one thing."

"What about it?"

"You let it out."

"Me?" Joe was dumbfounded. "I didn't! Who said so?"

Still she shrank away. "Master Tiberius saw you do it."

Joe felt a rush of anger in his chest. "That's a lie!

You know what Tiberius is like, Arethusa!"

To his surprise, she sprang towards him and pressed her hand over his mouth. "Sssssh!" she hissed frantically. "Someone will hear you. If they find me talking to you, you've no idea ..." Her eyes filled with tears. She held her hand over his mouth a moment longer, until she was sure he understood.

"You mean they'll punish you?" Joe whispered.

She nodded. "It'll be like Septimus, only worse."

"The scribe?"

"Yes. They found out he wrote the letter for Miss Lucilia - the story about you being Master Valentinian." She was trembling.

"What happened to him?" Joe asked.

"They were going to kill him."

Joe felt the blood drain from his head. "They can't do that!" He steadied himself against the linen racks.

"Of course they can!" The tears spilled down Arethusa's cheeks. "He was just a slave. We're disposable."

Joe shuddered. "You said they were going to kill him. Did they change their minds?"

"Miss Lucilia pleaded with her father not to. So he sold Septimus instead."

"Thank God for that!" Joe exclaimed.

"You can thank who you like," Arethusa said bitterly. "It left his wife without a husband and his children without a father."

"He had a family?"

Arethusa looked at him. Her eyes were lifeless. "Slaves marry other slaves. We're human too, you know." She began to weep. "His wife and children will always be slaves in this house, but they'll never see him again. He may just as well be dead, for all the difference it makes!"

Joe let go of her arm and stepped back. He had caused this. Just by being here, he had ruined the lives of a whole family.

"If they ever find out that I helped you, they'll have me killed," Arethusa sobbed. "They spared Septimus. They won't be lenient again."

Joe hung his head. "I'm sorry, Arethusa. I didn't realise."

She turned to go.

"Wait!" Joe said. "There's one more thing!"

She hesitated.

"Please, Arethusa! I promise I'll never speak to you again. But before you go, can you tell me, is Lucy alright? Where is she?"

Arethusa didn't turn round. "Miss Lucilia?" She swallowed a sob.

Joe held his breath.

"She's in the sanatorium."

Before he could ask what was wrong with Lucy or where the sanatorium was, Arethusa hurried away down the passage.

Joe stepped back into the linen cupboard and sat

down on his pile of sheets. This was even worse than he'd feared. If Lucy was in the sanatorium, she was either ill or injured. And if Lucy's father believed that he had released the leopard, then he was in very great danger. Fear churned in his stomach.

He thought hard. If he was going to survive here for any time at all, he would need some kind of disguise. Arethusa wouldn't help him again, and there was nobody else he could ask.

Suddenly, inspiration came to him. Didn't they say that the best place to hide was right under the noses of the people looking for you? Lucy had told him once that there were over a hundred slaves working in the palace compound. She didn't know them all, and hopefully nobody else in the family knew every single one either. If he pretended to be a slave, he might pass unnoticed for a while at least. And even if one of the slaves realised that there was an imposter among them, they might not raise the alarm straight away. It was a gamble, but he couldn't see any other way of doing it.

He opened the door to the linen cupboard and peeped out into the passage. There was nobody around, although he could hear a steady murmur of voices further away. He stepped out.

The first task was to make himself dirtier than he was at the moment. The boy slaves wore quite similar clothes to the ones he had on, only they usually looked grubbier and more worn out. As he went along the passage, he stooped to trail his hands through the dust down either side of the floor, and rubbed them on his tunic.

At the end of the corridor, he came to the room where the slaves had been cleaning the dishes on his first visit. There was nobody in here, but the door to outside was ajar, and there was a stack of earthenware pots on the side, as though someone was coming back to collect them. He would have to be quick.

He looked around. There was ash in the grate of the oven and soot in its chimney. He rubbed his hands in it, then dabbed his face.

His clothes were probably dirty enough from the dust and he didn't want to overdo it, but he dipped his fingers in the dish of a tallow lamp which stood on the side, and made a few grease marks on his tunic.

He looked down at himself. This was a good start. What he needed now was one of the dark aprons that all the male slaves wore, and a tray or basket, or some other prop to carry. He wondered about taking the pots from the side. But if the other slave came back and found them gone, they would know someone had been here.

On the floor beside the oven was a stack of logs. That would do for now, at least to get him as far as the back of the north wing. He'd seen laundry spread out to dry over bushes there, though he wasn't sure it had included the aprons. He picked up as many logs as he could carry, and let himself out of the door at the end of the building, praying he wouldn't be spotted.

Outside, the colonnades were a hive of activity. He hesitated for a moment. This was much busier than a normal day, more like the preparations for the feast. People ran hither and thither carrying all manner of things. But the work was being done in near silence. The faces he looked at were tired and worried.

He set off along the back of the west wing with his load, and had almost reached the end of the north wing before the log on the top of the pile rolled off. Joe crouched down, still holding the rest of the logs, and tried to shift them to one arm so that he could pick up the fallen one. As he reached down, however, the next two toppled off.

"What are you doing, boy?" A man strode towards him. "Where are you taking those?"

"To the sanatorium, Sir," Joe mumbled. His guts knotted themselves together in fright.

"You're in the wrong place, you do know that? And where's your apron?"

Joe stared downwards. The apron the man was wearing looked to be made of leather. "It got ... oil spilt on it yesterday evening."

"The first thing you should have done this morning was to get a new one!" The man glowered. "We can't afford mistakes. You know quite well that we've very little time to get everything ready."

Joe bowed his head. "Sorry, Sir."

"And look at the state of your clothes! Don't you

think the laundry has enough to do without having to provide you with clean clothes for this evening? If I catch you doing something like that again, it'll be the lash for you."

"Sorry, Sir," Joe mumbled again.

"What's your name?"

Joe gulped. "Privatus, Sir."

"Well, Privatus, pick up your logs, and get yourself to the store rooms!" The man jerked his head towards the back of the north wing.

Joe knelt down and carefully stacked the wood into the crook of his arm. His legs shook as he straightened up.

"Get a move on!" called the man after him.

Joe stumbled away, clutching the logs to his chest. Behind the north wing, he looked covertly around. People ran in and out of all the buildings, but he had no idea which one was the storeroom.

Just then, he saw a man come out of a barn, tying the strings of an apron behind him. Joe hurried over, dropped the logs in a pile beside the door, and darted in.

Inside, racks and racks of shelving were lined up across the room, filled with things like bundles of sacking, reels of wool and thread, and crates of all different sizes. All kinds of things were hung from the rafters too, including an enormous stag, tied up by its hooves at one end. The smell of ripe meat filled the air.

The aprons were hung over pegs on the back

wall in three sizes, small, medium and large. Joe helped himself to a small one. But as he put the loop over his head, a voice croaked out behind him.

"Where's your ticket?"

Joe spun round.

"You can't just come in here and help yourself to what you fancy." Sitting on a crate beside the door was an old man. He must have watched Joe come in.

"I h-haven't got one," stuttered Joe.

"No ticket, no apron!" The old man gave a toothless cackle.

"Where do I get a ticket?"

"Should have been given one when you handed the other apron in."

"I didn't. That is, I didn't get one. I was told to come straight here."

"Who by?" The old man narrowed his eyes.

Joe shook his head. "I'm afraid I'm new here. I don't know his name. A big man, a bit bald."

The old man harrumphed. "Probably Primus. Go on then, this once. But I'll not turn a blind eye again!"

"Thank you!" Joe decided to take a chance. "Umm ... I've got to take some logs round to the sanatorium, but I don't know where it is. Everyone's so busy out there, I don't know who to ask."

The old man clicked his tongue against his empty gums. "You youngsters! It takes so long to show you the ropes, it's hardly worth it." He took a stick and scratched lines on the floor. "We're here. The north wing is here. This is the east wing. And the sanatorium is here: northern end of the east wing. Got it?"

"Yes, thank you." Joe was about to go, but the old man went on speaking.

"The young lady of the family is there, you know. Has been for months. They say she's been seeing things, possessed by evil spirits or such like."

Joe tied his apron and looked away.

"Sad," the old man said. "She was such a bright little thing." He fell silent, lost in thought.

Joe stepped out quickly. Dread was building inside him. All the time he'd been sitting at home, telling himself to get on with his life and stop thinking about Lucy, she had been shut up like a prisoner. While he'd been worrying about what was going to happen to her father at some unspecified time in the future, she had been locked away for day after day. Months, the old man had said. Joe wondered how much time had passed here.

The worst of it was that her imprisonment wasn't because she'd been hurt by the leopard. It was because of him. He knew he had to get her out! He just didn't know how he would do it.

He collected his logs again and hurried round to the sanatorium.

"Yes?" The nurse looked up from her chair in the outer room.

"I've been told to build up the fire for the

patient," Joe murmured.

"I decide what she needs," the woman said acidly, "with reference to the doctor if necessary."

"The order comes from her father," Joe said, keeping his head bowed.

"I don't know how he'd know what she needs. He hasn't visited since last week."

"Should I go and tell him ..." Joe let his words hang in the air and turned to leave.

"No!" answered the woman hastily. "Do as you've been instructed." She nodded towards a curtained doorway.

The room beyond was like a cell, with nothing more than a bed, a chair, and a small stove. Lucy lay there in the half-light. She seemed to be asleep. Joe looked at her. She was pale, and much thinner than when he last saw her. She didn't look at all well.

As quietly as he could, he put the logs down one by one beside the stove. When he turned back to her, her eyes were open. But there was no alertness in them.

"Hello, Lucy," he whispered.

A flicker of life dawned in her face. She turned her head to look at Joe, blinked, and promptly burst into tears.

15

At the sound of Lucy's crying, the nurse came running. "What is it, Miss Lucilia?"

The woman didn't sound at all sure of herself now, Joe thought. In fact, she sounded nervous. He wondered why. He busied himself with stoking the fire, keeping his back turned towards them.

"Is it the boy?" the nurse asked. "He'll be gone in a moment. Or I can send him away now."

"No, no," Lucy wept. "I just don't feel very well. Could you bring me a decoction of lettuce?"

"Of course, Miss." The nurse rushed out at once.

Joe shut the stove and stood up. "That was an impressive show!" He grinned at Lucy. "What's a decoction? Is it like a concoction? I don't think I fancy one made with lettuce." He pulled a face.

But Lucy didn't stop crying.

For a second or two, Joe stood watching her tears fall, not sure what to do. Then he put his arms awkwardly around her. "It's alright. I'm here now," he murmured. "I'm going to get you out of here, somehow."

Lucy sobbed against his arm. "I'm so glad you've come at last. Oh Joe! It's been awful!"

"Are you ill?"

"No. Or at least I wasn't, when they put me in here. I don't feel very well now, but that's because they hardly give me anything to eat."

"How long have you been here?"

"I don't know." She began to wail again. "It was the day after the feast, but I don't know how long ago that is. I lost count. It feels like forever!"

"And you haven't been out at all?"

"No. They haven't even let me get out of bed except to use the pot. They never open the curtains, so I haven't seen the sky. I haven't seen my family. It's like being in a prison!" Her voice was getting higher and higher. "And the doctor makes me take this horrible medicine that burns my throat. I think they're trying to poison me!"

Joe stared. "Why are they doing all this, if there's nothing wrong with you?"

"They think I'm mad. Even the nurse is frightened of me. My father comes once every few days, just for five minutes, to see if I'm better."

"But how can you prove to him you're better, if there was nothing wrong in the first place?"

"I don't know!" She howled again. "I don't know what he wants me to say or do. But I'm so lonely and so bored. If I don't get out of here soon, I really will go mad!"

Joe squeezed her hand. "We'll think of something," he said, trying to be reassuring. "We've always come up with something before. You're so good at that."

"Yes, and look where it's got me!" Lucy wept bitter tears.

Joe stroked her hair. She was right. Both times he'd disappeared, it was she who had been punished.

"So what happened, after I went?" he asked. "Did they catch the leopard? Was anyone hurt? Did the wedding go ahead? Did they find out I wasn't Valentinian?"

Lucy waved a hand weakly. "Just ... hang on ..."

"Sorry. Too many questions."

She took a deep breath and struggled to sit up, but fell back against the pillows. Joe was shocked. She was so frail. There was no way he would be able to move her very far. Even if they could distract the nurse for long enough to get Lucy out of bed, it looked as though she would collapse before she got to the door.

For a few seconds, she lay motionless. Then she started to speak again, very quietly.

"The guards killed the leopard," she said, "but it had already attacked two of the guests. The woman died the same night. She had a huge gash in her neck. But I think the man survived." She paused. "Someone else was trampled to death in the panic as well."

"That's terrible! So did someone deliberately let it out?"

Lucy gave the faintest of shrugs. "Tiberius said it was you, and nobody would believe me when I said it wasn't, especially as you'd vanished by then. I don't know. Maybe he did it."

She was quiet for a moment, summoning her strength. Then with a colossal effort, she managed to sit herself up. Joe tucked her pillows in behind her.

"I don't think it was Tiberius," he said. "He couldn't wait for Marcus Placidius to speak to your father so that I would get found out."

Lucy nodded. "You're probably right. As it was, he ended up having to wait quite a while for that."

"Did the wedding still happen?"

"No. At first they just put it off. They thought it would be unlucky, since two people had died and lots more had been hurt. And then the next day, my uncle's family in Rome withdrew from the agreement. You remember they'd sent the leopard. It caused such disaster and humiliation for my father, they felt the only honourable thing to do was to back out."

"So Sallustia escaped the horrible stepson?"

Lucy smiled wanly. "It was a good day for her in the end." Then her face fell. "Of course, they'll be looking for someone else, unless they've done it while I've been in here. Nobody tells me anything."

"When did your parents realise I'd gone?"

"It wasn't until the day after the feast, what with

all the chaos. But then there was an inquisition. My mother had spoken to Severina Orbiana, who of course wasn't ill at all, so they wanted to know who'd made up your story."

"How did they work out that it was you?"

"Tiberius," Lucy said flatly. "He guessed half of it, and made up the rest, including the bit about you letting the leopard out. He made sure Septimus was punished too."

Joe nodded. "Arethusa told me that."

Lucy shuddered. "She was the only part he didn't work out, thank heavens."

There was a sound beyond the curtain.

"Quick! That's the nurse," Lucy whispered. "You'll have to go. Can you bring me some food? She has a nap just after the midday meal. You can creep past her then."

Joe bent and riddled the stove as the nurse entered.

"Still here?" She gave him a look.

"It wasn't drawing very well," Joe muttered. "It's fine now."

"I don't want to see you here again," she said sharply, "unless you actually come with the Governor."

"Very good, Miss." Joe slipped past her and out of the room before she could comment on him calling her 'Miss'. He had no idea how he was supposed to address her.

Outside again, he wondered what to do with

himself until he could take food back to Lucy. He would have to carry on pretending to be a slave, but the more people he spoke to, the greater the risk would be of being noticed.

He decided to go back to the room at the end of the south wing and see whether the earthenware pots were still there. He could carry those around the palace for a while at least.

Before he'd gone more than a few steps, however, there was a shout behind him. Joe ignored it and hurried on.

"You! Boy!"

He hesitated.

"Yes, you!"

He turned towards the voice. Lucy's eldest brother, Marius, was coming towards him.

"Have you just come from the sanatorium?"

Joe kept his eyes on the ground. "Yes, Sir," he mumbled in a deeper voice than usual. His heart thumped so loudly, he felt sure that Marius must be able to hear it.

"Is my sister still in there?"

"Your sister?" Joe looked carefully blank.

"Sallustia Lucilia, you half-wit," said Marius.

Joe nodded. "Yes, Sir."

"And how is she?"

He thought for a moment. It was so annoying to be accused of being a half-wit. But he knew it would be a mistake to let his cover drop. "I couldn't say, Sir," he said instead.

"But you saw her, didn't you?" asked Marius irritably.

"Yes, Sir."

"Well, how did she look then?"

Joe clasped his hands together. There was no need to tell more lies than he had to. "Thin, Sir. Not very well."

Marius shook his head. "What's the matter with her?"

"I don't know, Sir." Joe saw out of the corner of his eye that Marius was looking away. He stole a glance at the older boy.

"I'd really like to see her," Lucy's brother said, more to himself than to Joe.

"Why don't you, then?" Joe bit his lip. He had slipped up and said what he was really thinking, and in his own voice too.

But Marius seemed not to notice. "My father would be furious," he said unhappily, and walked away.

Joe breathed a sigh of relief. Thank goodness it had been Marius and not Petrus. Lucy's youngest brother would have been certain to recognise him.

He turned and hurried on. His best chance of not being stopped was to seem as busy as everyone else. Along the colonnades, people were still running to and fro looking anxious. He should have asked Lucy what was happening, he thought. And then he realised, since she'd been in isolation for so long, she wouldn't know anyway.

Suddenly, someone caught his arm.

"You, boy! What are you doing?"

Joe looked up at the woman. Her sleeves were rolled up and her arms were red. "I'm fetching some pots from the end of the south wing," he said, as humbly as he could manage.

"Forget that," the woman barked. "They need more pairs of hands to help with the accommodation."

Joe nodded.

"You know where Helena Calvina's suite is?"

"Yes, Miss." Joe bowed his head, wishing again that he knew the correct way to speak to female slaves.

"Where did they find you?" The woman chortled. "Well anyway, go straight there. It's to be rearranged for Domitia Longina."

"Domitia Longina?" Joe repeated.

"The Emperor's wife, you nitwit!"

"And the Emperor?"

"He'll stay in the Governor's suite of rooms."

"So where will the Governor and Helena Calvina move to?"

To Joe's astonishment, the woman cuffed him across the back of the head. "Too many questions, little big ears. Now, go!" She gave him a push towards the south wing.

Joe trotted off obediently in the direction she'd sent him, but his stomach was churning again. So that was what all the running around was for. And of course, the Emperor was Domitian, the same Emperor who was going to have Lucy's father put to death.

Joe's thoughts whirled around. Had he been called here to change the course of history? Was he supposed to do something to stop Domitian from killing Lucullus? Like what? Kill Domitian himself? He felt sick. Could he actually do that?

In the meantime, he couldn't possibly go to Helena Calvina's rooms. If there was one person here who might know all of the slaves employed by the household, it would be her. And she, of all people, would be the most likely to recognise him.

As he reached the south wing, Joe looked back to see if the slave woman was watching him. But she'd gone. So instead of going through the nearest door, he continued along the colonnade towards the western end, still keeping his eyes down.

Suddenly, a pair of feet crossed his path. Joe stopped just in time to avoid crashing into their owner.

"Look where you're going, you dirty little oaf!" snarled a familiar voice.

Joe froze. It was Tiberius. "Sorry, Sir," he said, using the same deep voice he'd put on with Marius. He bowed low, bracing himself for Tiberius to strike him. That would still be better than being recognised.

But Tiberius was gone already. "You'd better be!" he snapped over his shoulder.

Joe breathed again and hurried on. But

something was niggling in his mind. There was something about Tiberius.

He rubbed his forehead, trying to think. Then he realised. Tiberius had been holding some kind of object in his hand, grasping it so tightly that his knuckles where white.

Joe turned to see where he'd gone. It took a couple of seconds to spot him among all the slaves, but he was marching along the eastern colonnade. Joe's breath caught in his throat. It looked as though Tiberius might be going to the sanatorium.

He hurried after him as quickly as he dared, afraid of drawing attention to himself. He couldn't risk being stopped again and sent on another errand.

Outside the door of the sanatorium, he paused. From inside, he could hear the nurse's voice. "You can't just go in there! Nobody's to see her!"

"Hold your tongue, woman!" Tiberius growled. "I'll do what I like."

"We've been given strict instructions!" the nurse shrieked.

"Did you not hear me?"

Joe could tell from Tiberius' voice that he'd bared his teeth.

"Either you hold your tongue, or I'll make sure it gets held for you. Forever!" There was a sound as though he'd lunged forward.

The nurse squealed.

"Do you understand?" hissed Tiberius.

The woman whimpered.

"Now stay there, and don't you dare call anyone."

There was a swish as Tiberius flicked open the curtain in the doorway of the sick room.

As quietly as possible, Joe crept into the outer room of the sanatorium. The nurse sat in her chair, gripping the arms of it with both hands as though she'd been tied up. She stared at Joe and opened her mouth, but made no sound. He pressed his finger hard against his lips. The nurse closed her mouth again.

From Lucy's room, he heard a cry. "No! Tiberius, no! I beg you!"

He crept forward. He would only have one chance against the bigger boy, and the only weapon he had was the element of surprise.

Tiberius had his back to the open doorway. He was bending over the bed. "Don't worry, little Lucilia," he crooned. "I've sharpened it so that it won't hurt so much."

"Why would you do this?" Lucy's voice was barely above a whisper. "I've never done anything to hurt you."

"You haven't done anything to be favoured either, have you? Your father clearly doesn't think so, since he's locked you up in here."

"I don't understand. If I'm locked up, how could I possibly be favoured?"

Tiberius leaned closer. "There are rumours that

Domitia Longina is looking for a companion, a girl not yet of marriageable age." He cocked his head to one side. "I agree, it's very unlikely that she would choose you, now that we know you're mad. But you must see, you're the only girl who might do. Sallustia's too old, and Antonia is too young."

"Why would you care?"

"Because they'll only take one of us."

"But you're a boy! If she's looking for a girl, she wouldn't take you anyway."

"I know that, fool! But the Emperor might. Did you know," Tiberius said softly, "that Domitian's only son died when he was three? Had he lived, he would have been the same age as me."

Joe's skin crawled.

"As it is, the Emperor has no heir for his dynasty."

"What makes you think he would take you?"

"Just because your family doesn't want me," Tiberius snarled suddenly, "it doesn't mean that nobody else does! The Emperor is a man without a son. I am a boy without a father. We could be a happy ending for each other." There was no pleasure in his voice. "But only if they don't take you. And if I spoil your pretty face with a few cuts here and there, we can make sure that they won't want to."

He raised his fist.

Lucy screamed.

Joe leapt out from behind the curtain, on to

Tiberius' back. He grabbed his right arm and wrenched it away from Lucy.

Tiberius shouted in surprise and writhed round. Joe clung on, still gripping Tiberius' arm. Tiberius stabbed desperately behind him.

Joe felt a sharp pain in his thigh. He looked down. The iron shaft of a stylus stuck out of his flesh.

Tiberius seized the end and twisted it. Joe yelled. He let go of Tiberius' arm, and dug with his fingers into the older boy's eye sockets.

Tiberius screeched. He dropped the stylus and clawed at Joe's hands.

For a few seconds, they wrestled together in wordless fury. Then Tiberius staggered. Together, they fell, legs and arms entwined. The stone floor slammed against Joe's shoulder. His head cracked down. The room seemed to go dark. He blinked. Pain rushed in on him.

All at once, Tiberius let go.

In the doorway stood Lucullus.

16

"What on earth is going on?" Lucullus' face was thunderous.

In an instant, Tiberius had sprung away.

Joe lay on the flagstones, gasping for breath. His thigh throbbed. He wondered vaguely how the wound would show itself when he was back at home.

"It's him, Sir!" Tiberius jabbed his finger at Joe. "It's Lucilia's demon!" His voice rose hysterically. "She called him forth! He was trying to kill me!"

"No!" Joe and Lucy both shouted. Anger surged through Joe, lifting him on to his feet to face Tiberius.

"You were going to slash her face with that stylus!" Joe cried. "You've even sharpened it! I heard every word you said!"

For a split second, uncertainty flashed across Tiberius' face. "You liar!" he shrieked. He leapt towards Joe. "You evil, monstrous creature! Go back to where you came from!" His hands were at Joe's throat, grasping, choking, tightening.

"Enough!" bellowed Lucullus. "That's enough!"

Tiberius let his hands fall. Joe spluttered and coughed.

"You're bleeding," Lucullus said to Joe.

He looked down. The bottom of his tunic was drenched and red. Blood continued to stream down his leg, dripping onto the floor beside his foot. He swayed dizzily at the sight of it.

Lucullus shook his head. "You cannot be from the spirit world, when blood pours out of you, exactly as it would pour out of me. Nurse! Bring a bandage for the boy!"

The nurse darted into the room.

"In the meantime," Lucullus went on, "Lucilia will tell me what happened here."

"Oh yes!" Tiberius waved his arms around wildly. "Ask her, why don't you? Ask your lunatic daughter, the girl possessed by demons!"

"Silence!" roared Lucullus.

Tiberius flinched.

"I have wronged her," Lucy's father said, through clenched teeth. "She shall have the first word. I owe her that, at least."

Joe looked up from the nurse's bandage. Lucy sat upright in the bed. Her face was almost as pale as the pillows behind her.

"What Joe said is true," she said. "Tiberius was about to cut my face with the stylus that's down there on the floor." She sounded weary. "He wanted to make sure the Emperor's wife wouldn't choose me as her companion."

"What is this?" Lucullus turned on Tiberius. Joe trembled at the rage in his eyes.

But Tiberius had lost all fear. "The Emperor will take me, not her," he said belligerently. "He needs an heir more than his wife needs a companion."

"You may be right," said Lucullus. "But what on earth is there to recommend *you* as the heir to his dynasty?" He snorted.

Tiberius' face twisted. "That's just it!" he screamed. "That's the point! You can't see anything good in me! You never have done! I don't know why you took me in. I've always been second best! Nothing I've ever done has been good enough for you."

"What ingratitude!" Lucullus towered over Tiberius. "I've treated you like my own son. I've given you everything that I have given to Marius. And this is how you thank me!"

Tiberius sneered. "It hasn't exactly been a hardship, has it, providing for one extra person? Look at everything you've got." He spread his arms wide in a gesture which went beyond the walls of the sanatorium. "You live in luxury. Your family have an easy life. You want for nothing!"

"You, too, want for nothing, living here with us!" Lucullus turned away, disgusted. "If you remember," he said icily, "your mother's new husband wouldn't keep you. Not even your mother wanted you."

"She had my sisters," Tiberius said bitterly. "She kept them close, didn't she, her precious daughters. She didn't send them away, only me." He looked at Lucy. His lip curled. "Why would you choose girls over a boy? They have to be pampered and looked after, like pets. They can't even support themselves. They're a drain on society."

"Don't be such an imbecile!" Lucullus pounded with his fist against the wall. "The survival of the human race depends on them. And I'd like to hear you tell my wife that she's no more than a pet! She's the one who runs this household, not me! Over a hundred slaves, all my staff, the family, our visitors, every arrangement is taken care of, whether I'm here or not! Don't tell me she's a drain on me!"

Surprise flickered in Tiberius' eyes. "In any case," he blustered, "Domitian would do much better to take me back to Rome with him than Lucilia."

"Go on, then!" Lucullus rolled his eyes. "Try your luck with him! See if you can persuade him that you're worth more than the dirt on his shoe. I very much doubt it, but I'm happy for you to try. You'll be no loss to me after this."

"So be it!" Tiberius spat at the floor at Lucullus' feet.

In one swift movement, Lucullus crossed the space between them and hit him hard across the cheek.

Tiberius reeled back. "You'll pay for this," he

snarled. "You wait."

Lucullus shrugged. "What could you ever do? Just don't come crawling back to me when you fail."

"I'll see you in hell before I do that!" Tiberius cried. He whirled round, and out of the room.

For a moment, everyone was silent, listening to his retreating feet. Then Lucullus went over to Lucy's bed and took her hand. "Oh, my daughter. What have I done to you?"

"I don't know, father." Lucy faltered. "But what if Tiberius succeeds? What if the Emperor likes him? Imagine, if Tiberius became the next Emperor!" Her voice quavered. "It would be terrible! He's so cruel!"

Joe stood up and went to the other side of Lucy's bed. "He won't," he said.

"I doubt it very much," said Lucullus, "though we can't be certain."

"Joe can," Lucy said.

"So it's Joe, is it?" Lucullus asked, looking at him. "I'd been wondering what you were really called. Are you a Briton?"

"Yes, but not in the way you mean."

"What are you then?" Lucy's father sounded genuinely curious.

Lucy sat forward. Her dark hair fell on her shoulders. There was a little colour in her cheeks now. "He's from the future, aren't you, Joe?"

Joe nodded and blushed. Hearing it said out loud to an adult, it sounded so foolish. But Lucullus didn't laugh.

"Then, perhaps you do know," he said, thoughtfully.

Joe steeled himself. "I know that Domitian will be killed by his own advisers in a few years time. After him, the next Emperor will be a man named Nerva. Then there's someone else, and after that comes Hadrian, who will build a great wall. Tiberius will never be heard of in the history books."

Lucullus smiled. "How very useful! That's enormously more definite than the soothsayer I spoke to this morning. I'd called her to ask for predictions regarding the Emperor's visit. But all she had to say was that I had judged someone wrongly, and that I should put things right. I thought she might be talking about Lucilia. That's why I came in."

Joe looked at Lucy. "Maybe she did mean that," he said. "It was never Lucy's fault, the way I appeared here, and then disappeared again. The story she invented about Valentinian was only to help me. I know it was a lie, but she did it out of kindness, to protect me."

"Well," said Lucullus, "in that case, my daughter, I'm sorry that I've punished you like this. Please forgive me."

Lucy smiled and squeezed his hand. "Of course I forgive you."

Joe cleared his throat nervously. "There is something else I found out," he said.

"By all means. What else have you seen?"

"I haven't seen any of this - I only know what's written down in books about Roman history written two thousand years from now." He wound his fingers together. "You won't like it."

Lucullus looked him squarely in the face. "Tell me."

"You're going to die."

Lucy's father frowned. "Of course I am. We all die. Do you mean that I'm going to die of unnatural causes?"

Joe nodded. He found he couldn't look at Lucy. "Domitian will have you put to death." He heard Lucy gasp.

"I see." Lucullus was silent for a moment. "Do you know when and where?"

Joe hung his head. "No. It isn't recorded, as far as I know. But it must be in the next year, or two years at most." He wrung his hands together. "I wasn't sure whether to tell you. I don't know whether it's possible to stop it from happening."

Lucullus shrugged. "Probably not, if it's written in your history. It's what we would call fate. Do you know why he's going to execute me?"

"It was written down that a new kind of lance will be named after you, not after Domitian. He will be angry."

To Joe's surprise, Lucullus laughed.

"Why is that funny, father?" Lucy was on the

edge of tears.

Lucullus shook his head. "It's not really. If that's the real reason, it's absurd. And if it's not, and it's just an excuse, it shows that I can't avoid it."

He was thoughtful for a moment. "Come here, Joe."

With shaking legs, Joe walked around Lucy's bed.

"You have helped me, in telling me this," Lucullus said, placing his hands on Joe's shoulders. "Thank you."

Joe bowed his head. Lucullus let his hands fall.

"There have been rumours for over a year that the Emperor is becoming more and more paranoid. He suspects everyone of plotting against him. The more power he gives someone, the more he suspects them. He's already put twelve senators and two members of his own family to death. If I am put to death over the naming of a lance, it will be because he wanted to get rid of me, not because of anything I've actually done."

"I don't understand," Joe said. "How have I helped you?"

Lucullus smiled ruefully. "If I know my fate, at least I can put my affairs in order. My family will need somewhere to live, for example. They won't be able to stay here once I'm gone. I would prefer to arrange that while I'm alive, rather than leave them to take their chances when I'm dead."

"Oh, father!" Lucy burst into tears. "How can

you talk like that?"

"These are brutal times, my daughter." Lucullus sighed. "You don't know anything of what goes on in Rome, or on the battlefields of the empire. Even the emperors who we remember with admiration - even Caesar himself - every one of them has been responsible for many thousands of deaths. Our civilisation floats on a sea of innocent blood."

He took Lucy's hand again. "Domitian will arrive soon, and I must go and prepare to receive him. I beg you both to come to the feast, and sit beside me at high table. Lucilia, you shall have a public apology. And Joe, if there is anything I can do to express my gratitude to you, please tell me."

Joe hesitated. "Actually, there is something, Sir."

"Speak!"

"Septimus, the scribe..." He paused. "His family has suffered because he helped me. I heard he was sold. Would you be able to buy him back?"

Lucullus beamed. "I can do more than that. I will buy him back. And then I shall make him a free man, and his wife and children likewise. They need never work as slaves again."

Lucy clapped her hands. "Thank you! Oh, thank you!"

Her father shook his head. "I'm only glad you persuaded me not to put him to death. That could not have been undone." He kissed her on the forehead and bowed formally to Joe. At the door, he turned back.

"By the way, Joe, did you let the leopard out, on the day of Sallustia's wedding?"

"No, Sir." Joe put his hand on his heart. "I swear on my life that I had nothing to do with it."

Lucullus nodded. "I did think at the time it was rather convenient to blame the one person who was no longer there. Although given that you'd vanished, it seemed possible." He rubbed his chin. "I wonder if perhaps Tiberius was responsible. He was certainly very quick to point the finger at you. After today, nothing would surprise me." He left the room.

Joe sat down on the edge of Lucy's bed. She looked exhausted. "I'm sorry about all that," he said.

"All what?"

"I'm sorry you had to know about your father dying. I wasn't going to tell you."

She took his hand. "It was the right thing to do. It makes me sad, of course it does. But you have to remember, I don't know him as well as I might. In fact, I feel as though I know him better already because of what's just happened. Perhaps this will give us the chance to spend time together that we wouldn't have done. Who knows, maybe he will find a way to change his own fate."

Joe said nothing.

"Are you alright, Joe?" She leaned forward. "You look a bit faint."

"Faint? No, I feel fine."

"I don't mean dizzy. I mean, you look like you're

fading out."

Joe put his hand over hers. It didn't feel as firm as it should. "Oh no!" he said. "I don't want this to be over, not yet! I don't want to go yet!" He tried to hold her hand tightly, but she slipped it away from him.

"I think it might be time, Joe," she whispered. "I think perhaps you've done what you were supposed to do."

She reached behind her, beneath the pillow, and brought out his St. Christopher. "I've been keeping this safe for you. I couldn't wear it any more - the doctor would have taken it away - but I've been looking after it so that you could have it back." She held it out to him. "You said your father gave it to you. You should take it."

Joe didn't move, so she put it into his hand.

"Goodbye, Joe," she said. "Thank you for helping me."

He looked down at the silver disk in his palm and the cord she'd strung it on. He looked up at Lucy again. She was scarcely more than an outline, like a figure in the mist.

"Goodbye, Lucy," he said. "I hope we meet again."

There was a hissing in his ears. Her reply came to him as though from a great distance. "Perhaps we will," she said.

"I really hope so," he answered.

But she was gone and the sanatorium was gone. He was standing in his own bedroom again. He looked down at his palm a second time. The St. Christopher gleamed so brightly that it seemed almost as if a light shone out of it. The cord was gone.

He reached down to his thigh. He was wearing jeans again. His leg didn't hurt and there was no sign of any blood.

He sat down on his bed, despondent.

"Are you okay, Joe?" his mum asked, coming into the room. "Fed up about going back to school?"

Hastily, he stuffed the St. Christopher under the duvet.

"It's always a bit like that at the end of the holidays, isn't it?" she said. "Back to earth with a bump." She gave him a quick hug. "You'll slip straight back into it, you'll see. Now then, time for bed."

Joe got undressed slowly. In his mind, he was still with Lucy and her father. He wanted to be there, he wanted to see Domitian and watch Tiberius trying to find favour with the Emperor. It wasn't fair that he should have to miss all of that.

He pulled off his jeans. And there, in the middle of his thigh, right where the stylus had gone into his leg, was a round, pale mark. It hadn't been there before, he was absolutely certain. He pressed it with his finger. It faded and then reappeared again. He grinned. There was something to show for it after all.

That night, as he lay in bed, he put his hand

beneath his pillow to touch his St. Christopher. At the moment, he couldn't think how he would explain to Sam and Mum that he suddenly had it again. But that was a problem for another day. What was more important was that if Lucy was right, and it was the key to her world, there had to be a reason why she'd given it back.

Lying in the darkness, he felt sure that somehow he would find a way to see her again. He held the silver disk tightly in his hand. It was the only thing that mattered.

Maybe not now. Maybe not tomorrow. But one day, they would meet again.

WANT TO READ ON?

Turn to page 215 to try the next book in *The Scar Gatherer* series …

GLOSSARY

Ave!
a Roman greeting meaning "hail" or "hello"

Bene tibi!
the Roman way of saying "cheers!" or "good health!" when having a drink

bulla
a lucky charm, often golden and circular, worn like a locket, given to boys in Roman times nine days after birth to protect against evil spirits

caldarium
a hot, steamy room in a Roman bath house

cloister
an outdoor walkway where the roof is held up by pillars, often looking out on to a courtyard, such as you might see in a monastery or cathedral

cognomen
the third name in the Roman naming system, roughly equivalent to a nickname at the time this book is set

colonnade
a series of pillars along the outside of an old building, sometimes supporting a roof, like a kind of cloister (see above)

decoction
a way of making a drink or ointment by boiling up plants

espalier
a way of training fruit trees against a frame or wall so that the branches grow horizontally

frigidarium
a room with a cold plunge pool in a Roman bath house

Hispania
the Roman name for Spain

hypocaust
a Roman system for heating a room, where the floor was raised up on stacks of tiles and hot air was blown in underneath

laconium
a hot, dry room in a Roman bath house

lararium
a shrine in Roman houses where offerings were made to *Lares*, the household gods

mosaic
a floor covering in Roman times in which a picture or design was made with thousands of tiny tiles

nomen
the second name in the Roman name system, equivalent to a surname or family name

praenomen
the first name in the Roman naming system. Since there weren't many first names to choose from, people were known by their *cognomen.*

Propraetorian Imperial Legate
the person put in charge of one of the territories of the Roman empire by the Roman emperor

sanatorium
a hospital or sick room in Roman times

scribe
a person who writes things down or copies things that have been written

senator
one of the political rulers in Rome

strigil
a small, curved metal tool used by the Romans for scraping dirt and sweat off the skin

stylus
a writing tool with a sharp point, made from metal or bone, for scraping letters in a wax tablet

triclinium
a formal dining room in Roman times, where people lay on benches or couches to eat

Vale!
the Roman word for "goodbye"

Verulamium
the Roman name for St. Albans

wax tablet
a flat, rectangular piece of wood covered with a layer of wax for writing on

THE SECOND BOOK IN *The Scar Gatherer* SERIES

SAVING THE UNICORN'S HORN

JULIA EDWARDS

Saving the Unicorn's Horn

Chapter 1

Joe stood at the foot of the ruined tower. He glanced around to make sure nobody was looking, then swung his St. Christopher on its chain and let it go. It flew through the air and landed with a tinkling sound beside the high stone wall. He looked around again. Nothing. Nothing had changed.

For the last two days, he'd been swinging it and dropping it whenever he saw a bit of stone that looked really old, hoping desperately that he could somehow magic himself back into the past. It was two months since he'd last seen his friend Lucy, in her Roman palace, but the memory of the time they'd spent together hadn't faded at all. In fact, he felt like he missed her more every day. On the night before his eleventh birthday, he'd lain in bed in the dark, wishing and wishing that he could slip through time and see her again. If he couldn't do that, the next best present would be Dad moving back home, so that they could be a normal family again, like before. Of course, neither thing had happened.

But when he'd arrived here in York with Sam and Dad, for the October half-term holiday, he'd had a really strong feeling that he would find a way of getting back to Lucy, even though he was hundreds of miles from where he'd last seen her.

He picked up the St. Christopher quickly before Dad came round the corner. He'd been told off once already for being careless with it.

"You were lucky to get that back after you dropped it at Fishbourne," Dad had said on the first morning, as Joe picked it up from the cobbled street outside the holiday apartment. "You might not be so lucky next time."

"Sorry." Joe put it in his pocket.

"I don't know why you don't put it on. It would be much safer."

But although Joe had bought a new chain to replace the one that had been lost, wearing the St. Christopher round his neck would have meant that he couldn't get it off easily when he wanted to drop it. And since that was the only way he could think of for getting into Lucy's world, he would just have to be more careful and not get caught.

"Look at that funny old building there," he'd said to distract Dad.

"Ah, yes!" Dad nodded. "That's Tudor. Those big, black beams are always a give-away. So along this street you've got Victorian, Tudor, Victorian again, then -"

"What about Roman?" Joe interrupted. "Wasn't York quite important in Roman times?"

His brother yawned. "I thought you'd given up

on all that!"

"You're right, Joe," Dad said, ignoring Sam. "Roman York must be right underneath our feet. These cobbles are probably from a later period, but isn't it fascinating when you can see all the different layers of history in one place like this?"

Joe had agreed. It was just a pity, he thought, that the period of history he was most interested in was buried beneath all the rest.

He totted up now on his fingers. Since that conversation, he'd dropped the St. Christopher at least eight times without Dad noticing. But it hadn't got him anywhere.

"This is Roman, isn't it?" he asked, as Dad appeared.

"Certainly is." He read aloud from the sign on the wall. " 'Probably built in the third century, the Multangular Tower marks the west corner of the fortress.' " Dad looked at the stonework thoughtfully. "So that would make it something like 250AD."

Joe turned away to hide his disappointment. That was too late for Lucy. Even if she *had* somehow travelled all the way to York from Fishbourne - perhaps after her father had been put to death - she would still have been long dead by the year 250. And of course, if this was part of the fort, she was unlikely ever to have set foot here anyway. Why would a ten year old girl be wandering around among soldiers? No, this wasn't the right place either. It was incredibly frustrating!

"Shall we go into York Museum?" Dad said. "It's in the gardens just behind us."

"Can't we go to the Jorvik Viking Centre instead?" Sam asked. "I saw a poster. It looked really cool."

"It does seem to be very popular," Dad said. "There was quite a queue when we went past earlier. Let's leave it until later in the week, and hope that it's quieter."

So they spent the next hour looking around the museum together, peering at the objects in glass cases. Dad was just as enthusiastic as usual and Joe tried to lose himself in his stories like he'd always done. But now that he'd actually been there, back into the past, the stories weren't enough. He wanted the real thing.

By the time they had finished at the museum, it was late afternoon and already dusk. Mist crept up through the gardens from the river.

"Shall we find a café and have some cake before we go back to the apartment?" Dad said.

Sam groaned. "Can't we just go home now?"

Joe knew he was longing to get back and play on his new phone.

"No," Dad said firmly. "Let's go through the Shambles. That's another historic bit of York. It's very pretty and there's bound to be a café there."

As they walked back through the centre of the city, the streets were still busy. The lights in the shop windows were bright. Joe dug his hands into his pockets. Maybe it was worth dropping the St. Christopher one more time if he could, just in case.

The Shambles was a narrow street with old, crooked buildings down both sides. It was thronging with people. Joe paused, pretending to look in a shop window. Then, when a group of Japanese tourists were between him and Dad, he whipped his hand out of his pocket and dropped the St. Christopher on the pavement. It rolled into the gutter. Before he could catch it, it had fallen down between the bars of a drain.

He gasped and dropped to his knees.

All at once, his head filled with a hissing sound. The street was suddenly dim, as though all the lights had been switched off. He felt around on the ground. But there was no gutter and no drain, just a deep rut filled with muddy water. There was no pavement either. He'd done it! At last! He was back in the past!

He looked up, delighted. He was kneeling on a dirt track strewn with animal muck and straw, and mounds of rubbish like compost heaps. There was a smell of wood smoke, and another, much nastier smell in the air. He gulped, his excitement draining away instantly. It didn't look or feel like Lucy's time at all. Something must have gone wrong!

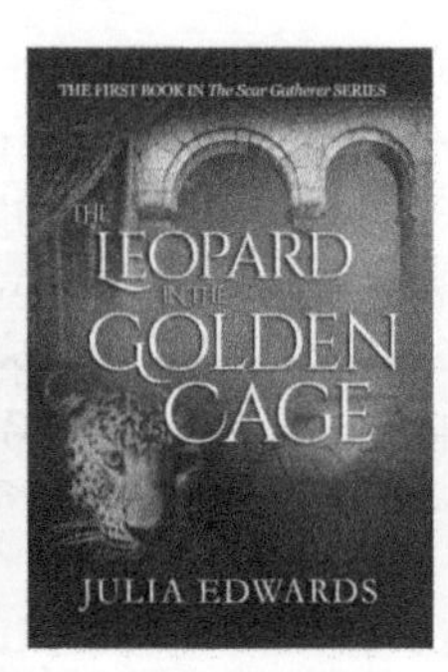

HAVE YOU READ THEM ALL?

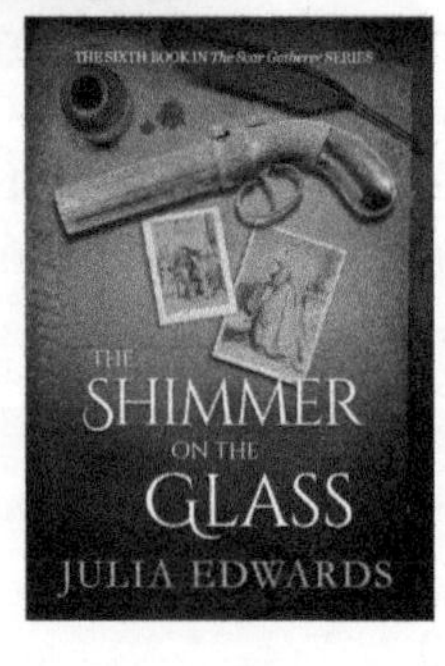